THE QUEEN OF SWORDS

OTHER WORKS BY JUDY GRAHN

Another Mother Tongue: Gay Words, Gay Worlds
Edward the Dyke and Other Poems
The Highest Apple: Sappho and the Lesbian Poetic Tradition
The Queen of Wands
She Who
A Woman Is Talking to Death
The Work of a Common Woman

JUDY GRAHN

THE
QUEEN
OF
SWORDS

BEACON PRESS • BOSTON

Beacon Press
25 Beacon Street
Boston, Massachusetts 02108

Beacon Press books
are published under the auspices of
the Unitarian Universalist Association of Congregations.

94 93 92 91 90 89 88 87   8 7 6 5 4 3 2 1

Some of the poems in this volume have appeared in *Zyzzyva* magazine
and Mama Bear's *News and Notes*. "Queen Boudica" appeared in *The Iowa
Review* and is anthologized in *Extended Outlooks*. Many of the poems are
available on cassette from Inanna Institute, Box 11164, Oakland, Califor-
nia, 94611.

Text design by Ann Schroeder

Library of Congress Cataloging-in-Publication Data

Grahn, Judy, 1940–
    The queen of swords.

    "Based on the 5,000-year-old Sumerian story of . . .
Inanna, Queen of Heaven and Earth"—
    "Second book in Judy Grahn's four-volume Chronicle of
Queens series"—
    Includes bibliography: p.
    I. Title.
PS3557.R226Q39   1987   813'.54   87-47537
ISBN 0-8070-6802-0

To my parents
Elmer A. and Vera D. Grahn

Finally, what you have to give
is everything you are.

Contents

Acknowledgments

I am especially grateful to Betty De Shong Meador for translating the original Inanna myth into poetry, and for being in my class these last two years, allowing me to bask utterly in the material (see appendix 1). Thanks to Mary Bradish for helping me get to my insides. Thanks to Barbara San Severina for her hard-won poem "The edge of death," which helped form "In the eye of death" in Gate Seven. Thanks to Lisa Beck for her bar stories, to Carol Seajay for vital discussions, and Mary Nordseth for her zany humor. Thanks to Willyce Kim for finding the ballads, and Kris Brandenberger for helping with the science and my "inner ear." I'm happy that Nancy Diuguid of England was the catalyst in helping to make "The Queen of Swords" become a full-blown play in addition to being a set of related poems. Thanks to Paula Gunn Allen for her discussions of philosophical ideas, including those of George Gurdjieff. Thanks to the Inanna group, including Karen Sjöholm and Elaine Blake, for listening and giving last-minute feedback; to Joy Harjo for loaning me her sword, and Katharyn Aal for her gifts of sword dance. Thanks also to Rita Speicher, Betsy and Sulieman Allen for supplying music to work by. I want to thank Joanne Wyckoff, my editor at Beacon Press, and the other Beacon people for their enthusiasm and respectful treatment, and for being a brave, bold, and fine press to work with.

For "Descent to the Roses of the Family" in particular I am grateful for the following help in the face of all our terrors: to the women of Common Lives/Lesbian Lives for printing it as a chapbook and for blessedly letting me have a large number of copies; to Paula Gunn Allen for helping me double-check my honesty, and for fruitful conversations; to Adrienne Rich for a truly artful critique; to Audre Lorde for helpful criticisms and suggestions for expanding the poem. Thanks to Michelle Cliff for warm and human responses in spite of her misgivings and to Joyletta Alice for strong support and then seeing through to a side she was able to use for herself. I want to thank Paula Ross and Marcy Alancraig, and the many helpful and supportive responses from Women's Voices Writing Workshop in Santa Cruz, where the poem was the primary subject of an exhaustive two-hour discussion between participants and myself. Others who helped: Carl Morse, Michael, Clover, Mark Thompson, Bob Glück (white Gay men) and the (black man) New York editor who said to me at a reading, "Never be defensive about this poem." I want to thank all the white women and men who publicly admit their similarity of affliction, and the black women and men who say, yes, it hurts and yet you *must* get it out there. As has been said so often before, if not now, when? If not me, then who?

Introduction

In my earlier book *The Queen of Wands* (first of four in a series of which this is the second) I began the saga of the goddess Helen, or El-ana, variants of whose name and story appeared repeatedly in European mythology as she ran for cover under the relentless authority of the all-male monotheism that gradually replaced her worship during these last few centuries. As Queen Helen she appeared in the *Iliad* where her abduction was the cause of the great Trojan War, when her husband Menelaus besieged that city for ten years with a thousand ships to get her back from her shepherd-prince-lover Paris. She died at the end of that story, murdered by her own niece and nephew as Greece overthrew its old matriarchy in a welter of blood, guilt, and grief.

But Helen did not really die, the story continued. Rather, she "flew into a cloud"—and will return to us when we are ready. In *Wands* I placed her as a worker (as all workers) in industrial capitalism and as a romantic figure in Euro-American folklore.

Earlier in this century the poet H.D., in *Helen in Egypt*, envisioned her in a haven where she could retain her old Hermetic knowledge. In the novel and subsequent movie *Sophie's Choice*, William Styron placed her in Nazi Germany, where she was tragically asked to choose between her male and female children. More archetypally, Gertrude Stein, in "Dr. Faustus Lights the Lights" in 1938, named her "Marguerite Ida and Helena Annabel," a character who says of herself, "I know no man or devil or viper and no light I can be anything and everything and it is always always alright." Stein apparently took some of Helen's multiple names from Goethe's *Faust*.

In a different story set simultaneously with the life of Jesus,

Helen and the great magician/wise man Simon Magus were worshiped together as gods under a plane tree, Simon having found Helen working in a lowly brothel. In a later and more chilling North European tale, the goddess of beauty entices unwary men into the woods by her astounding beauty; once she is certain they can never find their way back, she turns, and they see she is completely hollow inside: there is nothing there. Helen appeared many more times: as Elaine of the Celts, as Hel of the Scandinavians, as Cinderella, Snow White, Helle and Holde of the Germanic and East European tribal and posttribal folk, as Venus of the Romans. In a worldwide context her prototype is a weaver/fire goddess of fiery beauty and creativity with such diverse names as Ashketanne-mat of the Ainu people of Japan, Oshun, the beauty goddess of West Africa, Pele, the great Hawaiian volcano goddess, Skywoman with her tree of life of the Iroquois, and Chin-nu, the Great Spinster of China.

Sumerian texts of cuneiform writing, found at the beginning of this century and dating to at least 3000 B.C., have been unearthed at archeological sites in the Tigris-Euphrates river valley. From these texts, which are just now beginning to be understood, a great cycle of epic myths is unfolding. They center on the Sumerian goddess of heaven and earth, Inanna. (In neighboring areas she was known as Ishtar and Astarte.)

Practitioners of Jungian psychology, in particular, have translated and interpreted Inanna's stories, including the beautiful, lyric accounts of her sacred marriage to her consort, the bull god Dumuzi, and of her acquisition of the sacred powers of godhood, the *mes* (pronounced *mays*). For these stories I especially want to call attention to *Inanna: Goddess of Heaven and Earth*, by Diane Wolkstein and Noah Kramer.

I was especially fortunate when, just as I began working on *The Queen of Swords*, Jungian analyst Betty De Shong Meador joined one of my writing classes while she was translating into poetic form the text of a major saga of Inanna. This myth tells of her descent into the underworld, where she confronts its reigning queen, the goddess Ereshkigal (pronounced ER-esh-KEE-gl'). (Please see appendix 1 for Betty Meador's text.)

After living with this ongoing translation for several years I have no doubt that Inanna's story informed many later stories about the goddess-queen-harlot figures who are related to Helen, goddess of beauty and love. In "The Queen of Swords," I have chosen to depict the story of Helen, a modern-day Inanna, as she confronts Ereshkigal. Ereshkigal, the Queen of Swords, is associated in the Tarot deck with air, storms, intelligence, science, piercing violence, and strength. Among people who honor the queen of the underworld she has been called Cerridwen, the Morrigan, Morgan the Faery, Kali, Hel, Persephone, Oyá, and other names representing goddesses of death, rebirth, and the spirit world. She is remembered in our times as the wicked witch, jealous queen, or evil black-garbed woman who appears in stories such as "Snow White" or in comic books such as "Little Lulu."

I found it irresistible to present the relationship between these two female mythic characters, Helen and Ereshkigal, as a Lesbian saga, setting it in an underground Lesbian bar owned by Ereshkigal. The spicy Crow characters, Nothing, and the other naggy notables of the cast followed naturally. The myth itself is so powerful, however, and so profound, that it transcends any fixed setting or easy labeling of the characters. The questions it undertakes to raise concern the nature of life and death, darkness and light, innocence and guilt; how we human beings use the trials of life to transform ourselves from mundane to metaphysical and back again.

The Sumerian story upon which "The Queen of Swords" is based tells of the decision of Inanna, queen of heaven and earth, to go to the "great below," risking everything in order to gather even more powers for the benefit of her cities. She leaves her consort, the bull god Dumuzi, her children, and all heaven and earth in order to undertake this perilous journey. "Mourn for me," she instructs her faithful female minister, Ninshubur, "tear at your eyes and mouth and genitals." Then the great goddess makes her descent to the underworld. This domain, Ganzir, is described as a desert or wilderness; it is ruled by a shamanic queen, Ereshkigal, a Kali-figure of death and transformation. She carries a drum, is naked, stamps her feet, has hair like coiled snakes and long fingernails like "copper rakes."

Instead of a golden, jeweled throne, Ereshkigal has a plain wooden one. There are seven gates to her domain, guarded by a gatekeeper whose name, Neti, in Sanskrit means "nothing."

At each of the seven gates Inanna is stripped of one of her powers of office: her headband of queenship, her lapis lazuli necklace of rulership, her measuring rod, her man-enticing breastplate and perfume. Finally at the seventh gate she is judged by Ereshkigal's seven underworld judges, the Annunaki. Inanna is fixed by the "eye of death," and then Ereshkigal kills her, flays her corpse, and hangs her, like a piece of meat, on a peg. This complete reduction to "nothing" lasts three days and three nights, predating the Christian story of the Resurrection by several thousand years and giving us an arresting example of a female sacrificial myth. And in what to me is the most startling twist to the story, while the goddess of beauty hangs on her peg, the great queen of change, Ereshkigal, herself no simple figure, lies moaning in birth pains, apparently giving birth to a renewed Inanna.

Meanwhile aboveground the faithful servant Ninshubur goes to three father gods entreating their help in getting the goddess of love, beauty, and life out of the underworld. The first two refuse, saying Inanna asked for too much, and that in any event it is impossible to return from the realm of death. The third father god is Enki, god of wisdom and sweet waters. He is instantly sympathetic, and takes dirt from under his fingernails to construct two genderless creatures, Kurgarra and Galaturra. He gives them "the water of life and the plant of life" to take on their sojourn, as well as instructions for tricking Ereshkigal. They go down into the underworld, disguising themselves as a "cloud of flies" to get past the gatekeeper.

Standing before the agonized Ereshkigal, they commiserate with her, and their empathy tricks her into offering them whatever they wish. In true shamanic fashion they refuse to eat the deadly underground fruits that would prevent their return, instead choosing Inanna's corpse, and bring her back to life. Ereshkigal allows the queen of life to ascend, but only on condition that she send another down to take her place. Seven demons accompany Inanna to make sure she keeps her promise.

The demons attempt three "false arrests," including that of faithful Ninshubur herself, before Inanna takes them to her own beloved consort, the bull god Dumuzi; he is gorgeously dressed and sitting on a jeweled throne near his apple tree, not mourning or missing her. Inanna stares at him with her newly attained "eye of death," and the demons take him, though not before his sympathetic sister Geshtinanna offers to take his place in the underworld half the time. Ereshkigal accepts this compromise, and for six months of the year Dumuzi remains below while his sister descends for the other six months. Inanna again rules the world above, now with even greater powers. The myth ends with her acknowledgment of and love for the underworld queen: "Holy Ereshkigal, sweet is your praise."

Following this story closely I have set the play "The Queen of Swords" in a modern context, a Lesbian bar in which Nothing is the bouncer and bartender and the seven judges are Crow Dikes. (Crows traditionally accompany the queen of the underworld.) The play consists of three "aboveworld" scenes and seven "belowworld" gates. And in the spirit of the paganism that sustained this story for so long, I have made the play as funny as I could without losing its profound center of gravity.

The second section of the book consists of two poems, also based on the myth of Inanna's descent. "Descent to the Roses of the Family" is one long address on the subjects of battery, alcoholism, madness, and white and male supremacy. In the poem, a contemporary American woman narrator speaks to her brother about their parents (seen as Dumuzi and Venus), asking him to help her not repeat the same descent.

H.D. said that Helen gathered the white rose while her more violent sister Clytemnestra gathered the red. Rose Red and Snow White are figures in a Grimm story of that title, while the tale of Snow White and the seven dwarves opens with a drop of blood in snow. The image of red and white roses in my poem is shorthand for the loss and retention of a number of forces, especially "female blood powers." Fundamentally I think the Inanna myth is about menstruation, birth and death, that is, female blood powers and related male warrior powers which in the history of white patriarchal culture have been violently suppressed and denied for many centuries.

One consequence of this repression is the withdrawal of women into forms of passive madness, of men into mindless cruelty and self-hatred; another is the projection of passionate and mysterious power onto other groups of people. In the imagery of white supremacy, all manner of forbidden power is wrapped in the word "nigger" and projected out onto actual black people, who are then forced to carry the accompanying burden of scorn and punishment, as well as the ironic complete invisibility of their own personhood.

In trying to describe these dreadful phenomena accurately, so that we can free ourselves from their consequences, this poem stopped me for months, taking me down to the bottom of my heart. That is a good and necessary place to go, but I wouldn't want to leave the reader there, so I have selected a tribute to women's collective powers, hanging as they do in the balance of what is possible, to end the book. It is called "Talkers in a Dream Doorway."

THE QUEEN OF SWORDS

A Play with Poetic Myth

PLAYERS

MODERN NAMES	ANCIENT SUMERIAN NAMES
HELEN, *a modern woman*	Inanna, *goddess of heaven and earth, Venus*
THOMAS, *her husband, a scientist*	Dumuzi, *Inanna's consort, the bull god*
NIN, *Helen's friend and Higher Mind*	Ninshubur, *Inanna's minister, queen of the East*
NOTHING, *bartender, dealer, and bouncer*	Neti, *gatekeeper of the Great Below*
ERESHKIGAL, *Lesbian bar owner*	Ereshkigal, *Lady of the Great Below, goddess of the underworld*
Seven CROWS, *variously crows, dikes, Amazon warriors, motorcyclists, judges, demons*	Annunaki, *the seven judges of the underworld, also the Galla, seven demons*
PEN, *corpse of an Amazon warrior*	Penthesilea, *Greek name for the leader of the thirteen Amazons who fought at Troy*
ENKI, *god of the wisdom of nature*	Enki, *god of wisdom and sweet waters*
KUR *and* GAL, *vegetarian fairies*	Kurgarra and Galaturra, *genderless professional mourners/musicians*
GISHI, *Thomas's girlfriend*	Geshtinanna, *Dumuzi's loyal sister*

9

LIST OF POEMS

In the text of the play the beginning of each poem is indicated by a downward-pointing dagger in the margin. An upward-pointing dagger signals the end of the poem.

In a Glass House

Home of HELEN *and* THOMAS BULL. *With* NIN, *an ex-neighbor, now a friend. Nice house, nicely kept, somewhat fussy. Glass wind chimes.* THOMAS *has a telescope, set on a tripod and aimed through an imaginary window, upstage center; he looks out over the audience.* HELEN *paces behind him, sometimes looking over his shoulder, sometimes out a window at rear stage left, for her view of the skies. They are utterly detached from each other. Front door stage left. Stairs to upstairs bedrooms stage right. A collection of* HELEN*'s glass horses and other glass ornaments is in evidence. As* HELEN *and* THOMAS *are talking,* NIN *knocks lightly, opens the door a crack, peeks around, then comes in. She is carrying a brightly colored pouch.*

Each of the players in this play has an everyday modern side and a timeless, mythic side. Their costumes and gestures may reflect this. They act and speak naturally, not stiffly, formally, or "poetically." Their natural speech just happens to contain much imagery and to rhyme.

Helen

The sky is a sheet of crystal †
on a night like this.
I can almost see myself reflected
in its starry face.

Thomas

As soon as I have this tripod adjusted,
we can see her in her evening aspect.

Helen

I live in a glass house, with glass bells
and fine crystal,
yet I don't see myself reflected
in any of my aspects.

Thomas
> There she is; I've got her
> captive in the lens—
> how luminous she is!

Helen
> Venus shines expectant [1]
> in the embracing sky.
> A queen am I;
> Queen Helen is my office—
> loveliness and love
> are in my province;
> yet I feel a cloud across my mind, and ponder
> love and beauty toward what end, I wonder?

Thomas
> She's in good clear focus tonight.
> Yet—they say she is veiled,
> and they are right.
> Still, you'd never guess she was
> twenty-five million miles away.

Helen
> Venus of what universe am I?
> I live in a glass house
> with glass bells
> and glass horses;
> how rarely do I stand face to face
> with my own forces.

Nin
> The stars themselves, they say, have forces.

Thomas (not looking away from his telescope)
> Hello, Nin. Come on in.
> An electromagnetic net appears
> to stretch across the sky tonight.

Helen
> An electromagnetic network
> stretches across the sky—

as though space itself has a mind—
its own science . . .
What mind have I?

Thomas

Some fellows in physics
postulate other probable worlds
coexist with this one—improbable, eh?
For instance, what could live on this cloudy monster?

Helen

He has so many eyes to see things by;
he has glass eyes that magnify.
I live in a glass castle;
I feel so fragile
and unimaginative.
I have no expectations
except to shine . . .
I do have my beauty, my attractions,
but they're fleeting, fleeting
as the wind bleating in a wind chime . . .
What do I have to magnify my mind?

Thomas

Come look, have a last look
before I set up the camera for a shot.

Helen

I was a cherished, petted child.
I live in a place that's a crystal vision
from *House Beautiful* magazine.
I would expect to be very lively,
a vibrant person, so alive.

Thomas

She is veiled.
You can only see part of her at a time—
a crescent, like the moon. Even so,
she is so luminous
she hurts the eyes.

Helen
    I live in a glass house
    with glass bells and glass horses—

                            (She suddenly throws one glass horse to the floor
                                where it smashes. She is instantly contrite, and
                                    bends to pick up the pieces.)

    Oh poor horse. Oh poor horse. Of course
    I certainly didn't mean—
    to kill you—

Thomas (reacting to the noise, but not looking up from his telescope)
    What was that, Love?

Helen
    Oh, nothing. A little horse fell.

Thomas
    Oh, too bad. One of your favorites?

                                (He continues making his adjustments.)

Helen (returning to her own ruminations and pacing)
    Venus shines expectant
    then sets too fast,
    clouds erase her memory
    and shroud her past.
    A queen am I.
    Queen Helen is my office.
    Yet *trivial* is how I feel.
    Venus of what universe am I?   ↓

Nin
    Venus is currently traveling in Scorpio,
    but you look solidly earthbound to me.

Helen
    Oh, Nin. How are you, I'm glad you came over.
    The poor horse flew from my hand.

Nin
    Yes, I saw how it used your fury for a motor.
    I'm doing well, especially since

I moved away from here.
And I have a new vocation. Look!

> *(Holds out a long deck of cards.)*

I've become a diviner of the future,
using Tarot cards.

Helen

Oh, do a reading for me,
tell me everything that's wrong with me.

> *(She and Nin sit one on each side of a small table.*
> *Helen cuts the cards and Nin lays them out.)*

Helen

Don't tell me about tonight;
tell me about tomorrow.

Nin (examining the lay)

The card that signifies yourself is crossed by the Queen of
   Swords.

Helen (shuddering)

Tell me everything the reading means.
Is something awful going to happen to me?
Am I going to take a trip? I'd like to do that.
I really need some change of scenery.

Nin

The sky is a sheet of crystal on a day like this   †
a person could easily fall through
into an abyss.
You could find your astrological aspects
reversed,
your path crossed, your luck
cursed—
on a crystalline day under a crystalline sun
you could fall from this
familiar life
into some other one.
You could come untied,

17

open one door and enter another one.
You could begin this day with
a solid position in your class,
a marriage built on tradition,
an education, a vocation and an aim,
and having no further explanation than that
you fell through a sky of glass
on a particular crystalline day like this—
have none.   ↓

Helen (getting up, dancing around nervously)
You're right, it is time for me to take a journey.
And I must go, I must go wherever the wind takes me.
Perhaps out to a far mountain—to be a lumberjack!
Perhaps down to undertown, to have an adventure.
Thomas, will you wait up for me,
if I should be late?
Nin, will you still be my friend
when I return? Will you miss me?

Will the wind rattle the glass
in the window of your heart
and remind you that I'm gone?
Will you wait up for me, even if I'm late,
will you still be my friend when I return?

> *(She gathers up her purse, and as though packing,*
> *stuffs it full of various things: kleenex, her*
> *checkbook, lipstick, one of her horses.)*

Thomas (he doesn't turn around during this speech, but takes a camera from a case at his feet and loads it, reads the directions, cleans and adjusts the lens)
Oh Helen, don't go down   †
to undertown,
if you go down
to the underground town
you'll never be found,
nor worth the finding.
You'll catch some disease—

a venereal chancre—
and then who'll want you?
Who'll even speak of you?
Don't take such chances.

Don't go down
to undertown,
you're sure to be raped
and then who'll want you?
You'll give birth to an ape
or a pig-headed monster.
You'll have experiences,
you'll age, you'll wrinkle up
around the mouth and eyes,
you'll be despised!

Oh I'm just joking, but
Helen, really, think of your position
and your beauty. Like it or not,
beauty such as yours becomes a duty.
To save your face—and mine—
you need to stay here in this place—
and simply be desired.

Helen
Desire? And what of my desire?
And what is my desire?
Everyone wants Love to be his own,
to be her own.
But what is it that Love wants,
what does Love want to know?
Everyone wants Love to follow them
down their road;
where is it that Love wants to go?

Thomas
Oh damn, she's almost set;
I want to take a picture.
Love, bring me the lens cleaner, would you?

Helen (going to stairs, to Nin)
  I'm too nervous to stay and talk.
  I'm going up to bed; but tell him
  I've gone for a walk, tell him
  I've gone down below the horizon.
  Tomorrow I think I'm going out looking for a job,
  or an adventure, or something . . .

Nin
  Be careful out there in the streets alone.

GATE ONE: BELOWWORLD

Where Nothing Lives

ERESHKIGAL's *bar,*[1] *doorway and street stage right, bar occupying most of the stage.*
  The bar is rambling, has a back stairway and other rooms evident. The bar floor has two support posts with a large crosspiece beam that overhangs facing the audience, nearly center, upstage. If the set must be more simple, perhaps a row of coathooks on the back left wall, or a large standing coatrack with a sturdy base can be substituted. The main bar is mirrored and stage rear, persons standing or sitting at the bar turn so they are facing audience, the bar curves at one or both ends so it is possible that a person sitting at the end presents a side or even front view to the audience. There are two crossed swords over the bar's mirror. There is a small table and a chair or two upstage, center. A pool table is either down stage left or off left, with sounds of occasional games played by the CROWS. ERESHKIGAL *has an instrument she occasionally strikes, a set of metal, wood or stone wind chimes, or a xylophone that gives a similar deep-toned effect.*[2] *Generally the bar is cobwebby, garishly lit, seedy, and dusty-looking.*
  HELEN *has fallen and struck her head on curb or wall.* NOTHING[3] *comes out of doorway. Sign overhead says "*CROW BAR, ERESHKIGAL, OWNER." *Nothing is visible of* NOTHING *inside a long gray or black*

robe, no distinguishable gender, age, or, if possible, size; NOTHING
*wears a shoulder bag or purse of cloth that is obviously empty. In
offerings to* HELEN, NOTHING *mimes pulling things out of the bag and
giving them to her, and, though nothing ever appears in* NOTHING*'s
gloved hands, material objects such as glasses of liquor, flasks, bottles
of pills, drug paraphernalia, kleenex, etc.* do *appear on the table or
bar in front of* HELEN.

The seven CROWS *play several mythic parts, including crows.*[4] *As*
CROW DIKES *they are both butch and femme, aggressive, flirtatious,
sardonic, very physical and expressive with their bodies.*

Helen

Hello, anybody here?
I am alone.
I think I fell and hit my head
against that curb. I thought someone was
chasing me, some violent man. But maybe it was
just a shadow fell across me
made by the wind. You
have no idea how rough it is, out here.
Where have I landed?

Nothing

You're not *on* land, exactly.
You're in Underland.

Helen

I'm where?

Nothing

Underland is not a place like   †
"your land and my land," hinterland,
Herland, Thailand,
or even run-'em-out-of-here-land.
It's neither Disneyland nor Prisoner land,
nor of course Fantasy Eye-land.
It's not a movement
to go back to the land,
followed by "get off my land,
go back to your Ownland."

I know you've heard of Homeland and
Strangers in Strangeland, Wonderland,
Funland, Finland, Sunland and Overland,
and you're not in any of those places.
You're in Underland.
Here, give me your hand.   ↓

Helen

You're not easy to give a hand to.
Where are you?
Who are you? And what are you doing in that
strange outfit?

Nothing

You—who are you?

Helen

I—who am I?
I'm Mrs. Thomas Bull.

Nothing

That's more of a title than a name.
Haven't you a name?

Helen

Well, of course, my given name is Helen.
And my name is very often given.

Nothing

You sound as though
others often envy you.

Helen

Yes, I think that's true.
I'm one of the privileged few;
it's no reflection on you.

Nothing

I don't reflect easily.
Very few seek to be me.

Helen

Well, you—who are you?

22

Nothing

> I—who am I?
> I'm Nothing.

Helen

> You're nothing? What an awful
> thing to say. How self-deprecating;
> haven't you any self-esteem?

Nothing

> Being Nothing I don't need self-esteem.
> I find it rather limiting.

Helen

> Where are you from, then,
> who are your people
> that they let you be nothing?

Nothing

> I'm Nothing, from nowhere,
> and married to no one—
> I live alone here in the underground,
> when I'm not traveling.
> I live in a room with no furniture,
> lights, or heat,
> I haven't even a cat.

Helen

> Oh you poor poor thing . . .
> such a restricted life,
> Why—you're nothing . . .

Nothing

> Didn't I just say that?
> Why do you think of me as restricted
> when I'm welcome almost anywhere,
> I'm boundaryless,
> I'm often invited everywhere;
> there are so many wonderful places to go,
> when you're bound to nowhere.
> I live in the west, I live in the east,

I live in the north and south, the middle
and the up and down.
I'm here to be your guide in undertown.

(They enter the bar.)

Helen

But to call yourself "Nothing"
isn't healthy, it's putting yourself down.

Nothing

But Nothing *is* down,
Nothing is all the way to the bottom,
that's certainly the right direction—
it's where I can be found!

*(Helen surveys the bar, which also stops to look at
her, the seven Crows stopping their games to look
at her; then Helen goes up to Ereshkigal, a black-
and red-clad woman[5] who is ignoring her, wiping
a small table center stage that has a lit candle on it,
which Ereshkigal carefully blows out.)*

Helen

Hello, pardon me, do you work here?

Ereshkigal

I call it work just to remember who you are.
I'm Ereshkigal, the owner of this bar.
I'm surprised you got this far.

Helen

I'm glad to meet you.

Ereshkigal

You remember me, we've met before,   †
you passed me once on the streetcar,
pulled your skirts away, so they wouldn't touch me.
You didn't spit, exactly, but pursed your lips,
like this, as though you meant to;
and you've seen me glaring in fury from some picture
in the newspaper, taken in some jail, you've seen me
in the grade-B movies portrayed as a Mata Hari,

or an evil spy, or Mother Kali, or a spider—
a black widow. You remember me, I played your older
sister Clytemnestra once, in a violent Greek play.[6]   ⅄

Helen
Oh I have no memory of this at all.

Ereshkigal
Well, you, who are you,
that can't remember where you've been?
Who is it you think you are?

Crow Dikes (by turns and closely examining her)
She used to be the Mrs. Famous Thomas,   †
now she's Mrs. Helen Venus,
she's the sought after, hungered for,
she's the slobbered over, fought in behalf of,
she's the overly desired, envied, resented, bought,
she's the traded, stolen, lied and murdered over.
She's everything a woman ever wants to be, and more.   ⅄

Helen
I may be everything a woman
ever wants to be, and more,
but at least I'm not a bar owner,
or a madame, or a boy or a whore[7]
or whatever it is you do here.

Ereshkigal
Speak, Helen, speak into my ear!
Speak until your mind is clear.

Helen
I'm from a nice townhouse uptown,
married to a wonderful man who holds
a good position in science, and this place
makes me a little nervous, however
I mean no offense, I'm sure you're very nice . . .

Ereshkigal
Now listen, Helen, Listen with your inner ear.[8]
Be quiet, Helen! You talk too much![9]

Try listening, instead of such
a smokescreen of babble as you emit
to cover up your ignorance.

Helen

I have a certain problem with my memory,
perhaps you could help me, perhaps we have met
somewhere before, in some other bar?

Ereshkigal

Look, Helen! Look into your mind!   †
If yours is foggy, look into mine!
You were a goddess in Christ's time,
worshiped with Simon Magus under a plane tree,
doing miracles and acting like a Shakti,
and before that you were only a whore,
a working girl, a street queen,
found in a brothel where Simon set you free,
he and you together were considered gods— [10]
but before that you were just a whore—
and before that you were a real queen,
fought over in a great war; you were what
they fought it for . . .   ‡

Helen

Never, never, never mind. No use trying to remind
me. I don't have a memory of that awful time.
I live in a pretty house, full of glass bells,
I live with a man who does everything well,
it's just that I feel so trivial . . .
and I have a terrible time with my memory . . .
I set out to get better mental recall,
and to see something of the world,
and it's too early for me to go home.
Thomas would make fun of me
and then he would take care of me.
He must be worried, but I'll only be
a little while.
I want to go back—in style.

Ereshkigal
> Deny, deny, deny, deny.
> Seven venial virtues cloud her eye.
> Her first venial virtue is that she thinks she's
> something, when less than Nothing is what she is.

Helen
> How can you possibly say I'm less than nothing!
> I'm the goddess of love and beauty.

Ereshkigal
> Because Nothing is at least employed,
> Nothing is in great demand,
> and popular. Much more popular than you.

Helen
> Well, I have to work at what I do!

Ereshkigal (dancing with Nothing)
> It isn't easy being Nothing   †
> it isn't simple being down
> but someone has to do it—
> for the sky to turn around.
>
> We can't all be in our places
> in an orderly form;
> someone has to be chaotic
> for the sky to turn around.
>
> The wind is Nothing's true lover;
> where the wind lives
> is Nothing's true home,
> out on some street corner picking up crumbs;
> high on some mountain, down in the dumps.
>
> Where the wind lives is order,
> what the wind leaves is chaos,
> what the wind does is blow.
> What Nothing does is hold the place
> completely still, for Zero.
>
> It isn't pleasant being no one,
> the eye in the eye of the storm;

27

but someone has to make the spaces—
or the sky would never turn around.   ↓

(Meanwhile the Crow Dikes steal Helen's things.)

Helen

Oh help! Oh heaven!
Someone has stolen my money,
someone has stolen my credit cards!
Someone has stolen my identification!
Someone has stolen my coat!

Crow Dike Chorus

Five minutes ago she was a rich girl.

Crow

Mrs. Famous Thomas, wasn't it?

Crow

Lived on a hill.

Crow

Now she's a poor girl, no one.

Crow

Only has a first name.
She'll have to invent the other one.

Crow

Helen—Venus, isn't it?

Helen

Someone has stolen my shoulder bag!
Someone has stolen my picture!
Someone has stolen my fame!
Someone has stolen my position!
Someone has stolen my name!
Oh help! Who am I?
Oh heaven! Who can I be?

Ereshkigal

Well, what can you do?
We haven't much use for a pretty face here—
to stand around and look at you.

We're all pretty enough as we already are.
Can you dust?
Can you make beds others have rumpled
or do you just grumble?
Can you clean another's mess
and do it without a fuss?

Helen

Well, it isn't that I can't dust.
I just never thought to be doing it for a living.
A servant—Beauty isn't a servant—
trapped in housework—how can
I assert myself in the world?
Still, in this condition, I can't go home.

Ereshkigal

Listen, Helen. Listen with your inner ear.   †
Listen till your mind is clear.
Helen, you've been called Inanna,
a goddess, queen of heaven and earth.

How can you rule the seas
if you can't bait a hook?
How can love pour from your fingertips
if you can't cook?

How can you expect to
rule heaven
if you can't make a bed?
How can you affect stubborn earth
if you can't even bake it into bread?

How can you keep the order of nature
if you can't keep a simple house?
How ride the great breast of the wild wind
if you can't even dust?   ‡

Helen

I wish I knew what you're talking about.

Ereshkigal

Look, Helen! Where is your memory?

29

Look into your mind!
If yours isn't working, then look into mine!
You were a goddess in Christ's time.
And how can you be a goddess
if you can't even dust?

It doesn't matter what you sing—
as long as you can sing something;
and though it matters what you make,
it matters more that it be whole, some
entire thing, oh it really doesn't matter
what you can do as long as you can do
some things useful to yourself and others,
and the first thing
I want you to do, Helen Venus,
is to go get something for Nothing.
Then you'll be an underground Maid.

Crow Dikes

Maid in the Shade.
Yes, go get something for Nothing,
get it without being heard or seen.
If you can get something for Nothing,
you'll be a genuine underworld queen.

Helen

Oh no you don't, you can't fool me.
I'm not going to work for Nothing!

Ereshkigal

There is no use trying to think that way,
because here in underland
you do have to work for Nothing and that's
because here is where Nothing matters—
offer her something, Nothing.

Nothing

Welcome, welcome, welcome here.
You'll have a great time being nowhere.
Have a drink, have more
till you're falling on the floor,

have a drug, have a score
till you're crawling up the door.
If you don't want to go so fast,
I gladly deal in more gradual obliteration,
to the resultant obfuscation of obligation,
and the ultimate consummation of degradation.

Ereshkigal (playing her wind chimes)
It isn't as easy as it may seem
to poison the apple of self-esteem,[11]
and Nothing is the best there is at this,
Nothing does the job better. Nothing is tops.

Crows
Because Nothing matters! Nothing matters!
Nothing matters!

Ereshkigal
Nothing is sacred!

Nothing
Nothing makes a difference!

Crows
Nothing is important! Nothing is important!
Nothing is important!

> *(Helen holds her hands over her ears as the Crows
> dance raucously around the bar with Nothing
> while Ereshkigal rings her brass wind chimes.)*

GATE TWO: BELOWWORLD

The Nature of Nature

ERESHKIGAL's *Crow Bar, slightly neater than it was in Gate One.*
HELEN, *feather duster in hand, sits at the bar;* NOTHING *is behind the
bar.* ENKI *comes in, gets a beer from* NOTHING, *steps forward and ad-*

dresses audience. He is dressed in a gardener's outfit and carrying a rake and a duffle bag with clothes in it. He changes clothes during the course of the Gate to a woman's garb, makeup, wig; or perhaps he only puts on a long skirt, or a woman's hat. CROW DIKES *are sitting or standing around, playing pool and the like.*

Enki (to audience, Helen, Crows, and Nothing)

Where is when—   †
ever notice that?
When you go somewhere
has everything to do
with where you are
when you get there,
whether you're there again,
or for the first time.
It's evident
that place is time.

When is where—
ever notice this?
When you go too long
and too far
to remember where you are
or you try to meet
someone somewhere
in a particular space
and miss each other
by minutes
it becomes clear again
(or for the first time)
where is when
and time
is place.   ↓

Helen

I know where I am.
Here is where I am stuck in this underground bar.

Enki

Not only that, now is *when*
you've been stuck here in this underground bar.

Helen

    I've been left here with nothing.

Crow (to Nothing)

    Is she complaining?

Crow

    We do have Nothing to offer her.

Nothing

    You'd think she would be used to me by now.

Crow

    She can't help it.
    Nothing bothers her.

Helen

    It seems that all of humankind
    has walked away with me behind.
    How long I've been abandoned here
    even nature doesn't care.

Enki

    Who sits there
    describing her own sorry state of mind
    while crediting all of humankind?

Helen

    Nature doesn't give a damn [1]   †
    if I'm not or if I am.
    All the sounds of life I hear
    sound the same without my ear.

    Yet stars affect me just the same
    as if I were affecting them;
    and I love no less the sea
    for its never loving me.

    Butterflies and birch trees
    are unaware of pleasing me.
    Earth needs no love to give.
    We love. What other cause to live?   ‡

Crows

    CAW CAW CAW CAW

Crow

What other CAWS to live?

Crow

I CAW CAW CAWS to live.

Enki

Who's to say what Nature loves
and does not love?

Helen

Oh I wasn't talking to you.
I was simply feeling blue.
I long to get away from this ugly place
to go somewhere nice—to the country.
But I can't.
I'm reduced to nothing.

Crow (to Nothing)

Are you reducible, too, Nothing?

Nothing

Absolutely.

Helen

I have lost everything,
my name and position. I have to stay here
and be a servant.

Enki

That's what nature is—a servant.

Helen

You—who are you?

Enki

I am Enki, at your service.
I'm a gardener, of sorts, that is to say
I look after the natural world. You might say
I help to make its templates.

Helen

You're a very strange man, if that is what you are,
and this is a very strange bar.

Enki

    I like this place myself.
    Why would a beauty such as yourself
    descend alone to a place she despises?

Helen

    Oh, because I'm more than a beauty,
    I'm supposed to be in charge of beauty,
    but somewhere along the long line
    I believe I lost my own mind,
    so recently I set out to do more than stand alone
    in some admiring bask,
    I set out to do the harder task,
    to break, to ask,
    to fall all the way down,
    and eventually to understand.
    And I know I'm not entirely alone—
    Nature loves me, this I know,
    as she loves the flowers that grow.
    You, a gardener, understand
    how Nature holds us in her tender hands.

Enki

    Beware of little eggs that fall
    from Nature's hairy horny paw.
    What if it simply isn't true
    that Nature gives a royal damn
    if you're not or if you am.
    Who do you suppose you'd be
    if Nature didn't care at all?

Helen

    You say this to be shocking me,
    you must be drunk, but I'll be
    understanding—since you can't be
    nice, I'll do it for you. And I
    can't imagine who I'd be, if Nature
    didn't care for me.
    It's bad enough to live in towns

where mankind's evil brings me down—
the smoggy air, the ugly roads,
the huge inhuman buildings,
and the violence of criminals—
I couldn't stand never to sit
under a tree or to climb a grassy hill.
I get my strength from the wild land
and the wild sea, and my inner sense of
harmony.

Enki (to Crows)

Correct me if I'm wrong
but didn't she just say
she takes the strength from the wild land
to make up for her own weakness?
Did I hear her say that?
I've always called that stealing, haven't you?

Crows

We CAW CAW CAWL it CROWING.

Enki (to Helen)

Nature's all around a place—
a country home, a city space—
freeways have a nature of their own.

(To Crows:)

These humans strum a gloomy song.
They live in towns and run them down,
spin the gold from underground,
and then they say the area isn't Nature—
but it is—it's *their* Nature.
They simply have an ugly one.

Crow

This is Wisdom declaiming on the Nature of
Nature to someone who doesn't believe he *is*
Nature.

Crow

Not only that, he's declaiming on the nature
of beauty to someone he doesn't know *is* Beauty.

Crow

I don't believe in Beauty, either. I think it
happens only in the mind.

Crow

I don't believe you have a mind.

Crow

Well then I believe it happens only in the bowel.

Crow

You are a singularly foul fellow.

Helen

You haven't a woman's sensibility.
What could you know of Nature?

Enki

Perhaps I haven't any sensibility
except I know my nature and my name
and besides, in a way I AM Nature.

Helen

Oh what are you saying, you're lying,
who are you?

Enki

I'm the god of wisdom and wild lands
and fertilizing waters.

Helen

But look at you, in women's clothing,
boozing it up in this ugly place,
look at you—you're so *un*natural.

Crow

Who's unnatural?

Crow

Nature.

Crow

Well, that's only natural.

Crows

She's finally getting some sense.

Crow

What could be more unnatural than Nature?

Crow

Always interfering with the course of my life.

Crow

Always coming in here to drink beer and make a mess.

Crow

Always changing everything, ever notice that?

Helen

Men are so violent.
Woman is more like Nature.

Crow

women are not violent   †

Crow

and I am not violent

Crow

and the Queen of Swords is not violent

Crow

and violence is violet

Crow

and Americans are not violet

Crow

and the wind is never violent

Crow

and the sea, the sea is not violent

Crow

and nonviolence is not violent

Crow

nonviolence is inviolate

Crow

and the earth is not violent

Crow

and a shooting star is not violent

Crow
   and a volcano is not violent

Crow
   and war is not violent

Crow
   and violet is not violent

Crow
   and nice is not violent

Crow
   and nice is not viola

Crow
   and men are not violent

Crow
   and mice are never violent

Crow
   and the deer are not violent

Crow
   except in the woods

Crow
   where they live

Crow
   but in the movies they are not violent

Crow
   and the woods are not violent

Crow
   and puking is not violent

Crow
   and death is not violent

Crow
   and cars are not violent

Crow
   and Americans are violas

Crow

and violas are sometimes violent

Crow

and violas are sometimes violet   ⌄

Enki (to Helen)

It's your modern human nature to construct an ugly place   †
and then dislike it.
You weren't always like this.
Why do you go to the city of trees to help
restore your soul, why not do it in your own
city? Take a look around—
Here's Nature! Here's you!
Here's Nature and you!
It seems to me, at least presently,
and I have a number of opinions,
naturally, but currently
at least, it seems to me
that a beehive is a bee's Nature,
a stand of trees is a tree's Nature,
mountains have a rocky Nature of their own.
This bar here and this industrial city,
this is modern human's Nature,
you take your Nature everywhere you go.   ⌄

Helen

Oh you don't know.
How could you?
How dare you say cities are natural,
how dare you say I have no right to trees.
You—who are you!
You're only a gardener! A materialist!
Rooting around in dirt!
What do you know of beauty?
I AM beauty.

(Exit Enki.)

Nature loves me, this I know,
as she loves the flowers that grow.

40

Nature loves to give and give
and Nature loves—
what other cause have I to live?

Crow Chorus
  CAW CAW CAW   †

Crow
  What other caws to live?

Crow
  I caws to live.

Crow
  I live to caws.

Crow
  I love a just caws.

Crow
  I love a righteous and good and just caws.

Crow
  I loathe any kind of caws.

Crow
  I prefer first caws.

Crows
  CAW CAW CAW

Crows
  We prefer last caws.

Crow
  I prefer long drawn-out caws.

Crows
  CAAAAW CAAAAAAWW CAAAAAAAWWW

Crow
  I like edible caws.

Crow
  The caws of peas.

Crows
  CAW CAW CAW

41

Crow

The caws of corn.

Crows

CAW CAW CAW

Crow

The caws of war.

Crow

CAW CAW CAW

Crow

The caws of contemplation.

Crow

Contemplation has no caws.

Crow

The BEE caws—

Crows

CAW CAW CAW

Crow

The BEE caws—

Crow

bee caws of you—

Crow

there's a song in my heart—

Crow

bee caws of offal—

Crow

Bee caws of offal? That's awful!

Crow

Bee caws of offal there is food.

Crow

Bee caws there is shit—

Crow

there is grit—

Crow
    bee caws there is dirt there are trees—

Crow Chorus
    the mother of trees is dirt
    the mother of feel good is hurt
    the mother of all is none
    the mother of found is gone
    the mother of talk is breath
    the mother of laughing is death
    the mother of do is been done
    the mother of enough is waste
    the mother of more is must
    the mother of go somewhere is place
    the mother of beauty is memory   ↓

Helen
    The mother of beauty is memory?[2]

Enki (returning with another bottle, and by now even more cross-dressed as a female,[3] addressing Helen)
    You're wrong you know, that is, you're wrong
    in this particular place at this particular time
    and given who you're speaking to—
    the Wisdom and Nature god.

Helen
    Nature god? perhaps you have a thought or two
    on the nature of the Beauty god of Love and Life?

Enki (dancing)
    If you would be a goddess of beauty
    try first being a frog,
    something wet and green and viscous,
    something growing in a bog.

    First you need a tender belly
    and an all-consuming throat,
    fingers touchy as the top of jelly,
    an ability to float—

43

Helen

    Let's see if I have this straight.
    You're advocating
    nature as a building
    and beauty as a frog?

Enki

    I'm advocating nearly everything,
    and quite a bit of Nothing.
    What forms would you prefer we came in?

Helen

    Something pinker and more austere—
    something traditional, stars or
    sea anemones, or flowers . . .

Enki

    You see flowers as austere?
    You miss their rank indecency.
    I see a flower in its fullest blooming
    thickly musky
    as a woman with her legs spread
    for any lover,
    or a man with his stem sprung
    standing nude in the sun or street
    for anyone or dog to tweak.

Helen

    You aren't the kind of nature I adore.
    And my once precious view of Wisdom
    is hopping greenly out the door.

Enki

    We see things differently, obviously;
    through different lenses . . .
    Would you like to borrow my glasses?
    You see, on the one side is observation,
    and on the other—a crystal lens,
    for looking out and then for looking in,
    and not confusing the two of them.

(He holds out his glasses, she puts them on, then reels around the stage, examining people, walls, floor, liquor in bottles, her own hand, etc., reacting strongly, alternately shrieking, laughing, leaping, jerking, weeping, howling, in a rapid succession of extreme impressions. Exhausted, she wrenches the glasses off.)

Helen

What *are* these things—
they see absolutely everything,
from every point of view,
from lowest pit to highest summit.

(Puts them on again.)

Ugh. From many-headed microbe
to the interior of Nothing's robe.

(She shrieks at what she sees in Nothing's robe and jerks the glasses off again.)

Enki

Aren't my glasses wonderful!

Helen

They give me a giant headache,
and turn my stomach.
What are these things made of?

Enki

Lenses of the eyes of beetles and flies,
a dozen of each.

Helen

I have to give them back to you.
Oh Enki, I can't see from so many
points of view,
one is enough, or at most two—
I'd go mad if I had to bear witness
as thoroughly as you do.

Enki

I'm only trying to offer
a little clarity of vision.
Would you rather try my eyeball than my glasses?
It has a little more focus—eight miles, like an owl!
And you can see clear as a blowfish under water—

Helen

No thanks, no thanks, no thanks.
I really have nothing more to say to you.
Nothing! Absolutely nothing!

Nothing

You're calling me again?

Helen

Oh, I can't stand this crazy place.

(Exits to right.)

Crow

Nature offended her.

Crows

CAW CAW

Crow

She's a little coo coo.

Crow

And you're a little dodo.

Crow

And you're a little doo doo.

Crow

And you're a little ka ka.

Crows

CAW CAW

Crow

She can't stand being in this CAW-razy place.

Nothing

With Nothing!

Crows
Absolutely Nothing!

Enki
It simply isn't the nature of her nature!

> *(The Crows exit one by one pretending to be huffy,*
> *high-handed, and insulted by each other, while*
> *enjoying it immensely. Enki drinks a*
> *toast to Nothing.)*

GATE THREE: BELOWWORLD

Descent to the Butch of the Realm

Interior of the Crow Bar with ERESHKIGAL, CROW DIKES, NOTHING, *and* HELEN, *who leans her elbows on the bar facing the audience while the others carry on their usual bar business, pool playing, dancing cheek to cheek, playing cards, etc. Sensual music on the juke box fades out so we can hear the dialogue.*

Helen
I hate you all.
I came here with love, and goodwill.
Now I feel nothing.

Crow Dike (to Nothing)
She feels you.

Nothing
How sensitive of her.

Crow Dike
Do you think you're being objectified?

Nothing
Absolutely.

Ereshkigal
> What is it you say? Speak into my ear.

Helen
> I said, and I think I said it loud enough
> that even you could hear me,
> I came here with curiosity and goodwill
> in my heart, but now having been here
> a while, and being unable to leave,
> I have nearly come to hate all of you.

Ereshkigal
> Oh, you can't hate us.

Helen
> I can't? Just watch me.

Crow Dikes
> You can't hate us.

Helen
> I can't hate you?

Ereshkigal
> You can't hate us.
> We're Lesbians.

Crow Dikes
> You can't hate us.
> We're Lesbians.

Helen (fuming and then laughing)
> I can't hate you, you're Lesbians—
> what are you talking about?
> Of course I hate you.
> And of course I don't hate you.
> And of course I *can* hate you.

Ereshkigal
> No, not here in the underworld.
> Here in the belowworld Lesbians are loved,
> and Lesbians love.

Helen
> And what do Lesbians love?

Crow Dikes (by turns)
    Lesbians love
    to talk
    to sing
    to walk
    to cling
    to balk
    to sting
    Lesbians love to do anything,
    and to do nothing.

Nothing
    Not without my permission they don't.

Helen
    Actually it isn't hate I feel
    but endless curiosity.
    What do Lesbians do?

Crow Dike
    What do Lesbians do?

Ereshkigal
    Yes, what do Lesbians do.
    Go ahead and answer her,
    answer her true.

Crow Dike
    Lesbians love to do.

Crow Dike
    Lesbians love to dance.

Crow Dike
    Oh, Lesbians do love to dance.

Crow Dikes (by turns)
    Lesbians love to dance   †
    inside the thunder.
    Lesbians love to dance
    outside in the rain
    with lightning darting
    all around them.

Lesbians love to dance
all night in any
kind of weather, love
to dance up close
their arms pulled tight
around their partners'
backs and hips and
shoulders. Lesbians love
to dress in lace
and leather and
to court each other
(and each others' lovers).
Lesbians love to be so
bold and getting
even bolder, their fingers
love to linger
inside tunnels.
Lesbians love to dance
indoors and under
covers, Lesbians love
to dance inside
mountains and
to watch their lovers' faces
as they come and come and come
completely undone.
Lesbians
love to dance together
in the pouring rain, in
summer.
Lesbians love to dance
inside the thunder,
sheets of water
washing over their whole bodies
and the dark clouds
boiling and roiling like a
giant voice calling.
Lesbians love to answer
voices calling like that.

Lesbians love to
dance without their clothing
in thunderstorms with
lightning as their partner.
Screaming, holding hands
and turning soaking faces
skyward in tumultuous
noise and yearning. Lesbians
love to see each other
learning to completely
rejoice. Lesbians love
to feel the power
and the glory they can dance
inside of, in a storm
of their communal choice.   ⌄

Helen

Well, that's all very nice for you.
But what do Lesbians do that has anything
to do with me?

Ereshkigal

Look, Helen! Look into your mind!
If yours is scrambled, look into mine!
You were a goddess before Demeter's time,
Lady Venus of aboveworld form,
Inanna by name, Sumerian born—
you passed through seven gates of the underland
to deliver yourself into my hands,
into Ereshkigal's hands . . .

Helen

And you—who are you, really?

Ereshkigal

I am your wild cherry sister, red and   †
black sheep sister of the unkempt realm.
I am the Butch of Darkness and the Lady
of the Great Below.
I have a nickname: see if you can guess it.
Thistles in my fur are twisted

taut as wily wires of gristle.
You won't find me sitting home in front of TV
drinking beer, not me—I'm outdoors
prowling midnight. Nor do I march
to take back the night with other women
for I never lost it. My name is Shadow of the Wolf,
I woof and I whistle.
My usual companion-lover's name is "Destiny."
She had it tattooed
on my upper arm. She is, of course,
a Dike.[1] She chews me down to something honest
on a weekly basis when I let her.
Oh! But I have plenty of time for you
and your bright beauty—
yes, I have plenty of room for a Venus-type
such as yourself
in my chamber.
Remember me now whenever
you hear the phrase "wild cherry."

Oh descend
Descend to me
to my exhilarating gaze
and my desiring
Yes it is true—I am who wants you
and I hear you have chosen
to come down to me.

Strange to everyone but me that
you would leave the great green rangy
heaven of the american dream,
your husband and your beloved children,
the convenient machines,
the lucky lawn and the possible
picture window—to come down here below.
You left your ladyhood, your queenship, risking
everything, even a custody suit,
even your sanity, even your life. It is
this that tells me you have a warrior

living inside you. It is for this
I could adore you.

Now I want you to enter my stormy regions.
My gatekeeper will guide you; where
do you think you
want to go? Just ask his howling
hollow center.
His name is "Nothingness."
I want you to stand as I stand before you,
tremulous with expectation
as I reach to tangle all my fingers in your hair
to rip away the veil of your
perpetual smile, and then to strip
off your scarf of limitations, even
the birthright of your long hair itself.
Do my stark eyes surprise?
My name is "Naked of Expectations."

And I want to bend you
as I am bent to nip your neck, unclasping
your lapis blue necklace. Ever notice how it
keeps you from talking? You are going to do
a lot of talking. And no small amount of yowling.
Are you certain you should have come?
I may never release you.

Oh descend
Oh lower yourself to love
in the underground, the union
of a woman to one other
woman, not self to self
but self to other
self.

Slap your feet flat on the earth now,
heel first preferably, thrust
your pelvis forward.
You see I am about to change
your center of gravity.

As for those explanatory notes and diagrams
tucked under your arm—put them down.
You won't need them.
You will be too busy with your own internal
computations, as I lick between
your fingers, slipping off the golden rings
of definition and adherence.

Oh descend to me
lower yourself into yourself
as I go down
and go down
and go down to you.

I want you to fall, as I fall
heavy lying next to you, your twin egg stones
happy underneath my hands, the
pearl-pearl buttons I'm unsnapping,
then that thick-ribbed brassiere that gives you
all the cleavage you have used to
get your men to hope and grope
bearing gifts and favors.
You are your own gift now,
and you have chosen to come to me.

I of the snarled hair, the one earring
and the brassy metallic nailpolish,
I am your wild cherry sister. I am savage,
living in regions ruled by laws
that to you just happen.
When you say "just happen"
you will remember me.

I want you to crawl
unravelling
as I crawl over your dancing belly
to unbuckle the belt of willingness,
last obstacle before you splay your doorway
to my doorway. Reveal to me.
You have a secret self, don't you?

Can you bear your heart to be split
open and to lie so naked
in the sight of
either one of us?

Oh descend to me
mound on mound of Venus meeting
maddened Earth to be unbound on.
Fix your gaze upon me
while I find and flay you
with my fingers and my tongue.

My tongue is nicknamed
"Say Everything."
She's appealing enough
at first until she nails you fast
to solid dirt of the fat earth
and ends your fantasy.

You will moan, Inanna
you will cry.
Everyone you ever were
will die,
while you go down
and go down
and go down
on me.

Hanging helpless on a peg of feeling
as I bear you to your
new and awe-ful place of being, locked in
dead heat, we will argue. We will
fight. Your heart will ooze like red meat.
I will suffer too, to birth you,
to transform and finally release you.
I am cruel, yes. Exacting and not
possibly fooled.[2]
Pain opener. You want pity for your
little yellow egg of being
broken on my greasy griddle.

I am pitiless. And stirring
I will sear you, so when
next you say "you puking, putrid
lying self-conceited wretch you"
it is my face you will see,
my name you screech out "Oh! I'll Kill!
That Rotten! Bitch!"

Yes, I am the Butch of the Realm, the Lady
of the Great Below. It is hard for me
to let you go.
When next you say "you bitch"—"wild cherry"—
and "it just happens"—
you will think of me
as she who bore you to your new and lawful
place of rising,
took the time and effort
just to get you there
so you could moan Inanna
you could cry
and everyone you ever were
could die.[3]

> (A pause. Ereshkigal and Helen embrace, then are
> surrounded by the Crow Dikes, who hum a love
> song to them. All collapse to floor.)

GATE FOUR: BELOWWORLD

Amazon Rising from the Dust

ERESHKIGAL's *Crow Bar as before.* HELEN *is alone center stage. The
bar looks somewhat better than it did in Gate Three, a little decorated
and not exactly cheery, but at least neat and clean. She has been
washing the bar and mirror with rags, a bucket, a spray bottle. Her
hair is tied up in a scarf. She is tired from her efforts, and primps in*

the bar mirror, then goes to sit at the table upstage. Just as she starts
to sit down, she is startled to see a large waddy-looking mass just right
of center stage.

Helen

What dreadful thing is lying there
as though growing from the floor?

> *(Corpse of Pen gradually rises from the floor. She*
> *looks like a 3,000-year-old corpse, yet underneath*
> *the torn flesh, rotten garments, and protruding*
> *bones, Pen is actually quite handsome and would*
> *be appealing to Helen if she were an entire being.*
> *She rises, holding one arm up first, fist clenched,*
> *and then the first shoulder while she braces herself*
> *with her other hand, teeth wrenched over her*
> *tongue, the flesh pulled tight over her*
> *skull to form a human face.)*

Pen

I am not graceful in this first movement.

Helen

You—who are *you?*

Pen

I have been the Amazon   †
in the dust.
From dust all things arise.
I'm a little awkward getting up.

Helen

Don't bother, then.
Just sit where you are,
at least until you have your face on.
You look like a pile of bones
from some garbage pit.

Pen (sarcastically, and rising anyway)

Thanks a lot.
The last time we met
was during the great war.

Helen

The First World War?

Pen

Not that one,
the earliest one, the war at Troy
three thousand years ago.
You had gone there to be with Paris
of your own choosing.
We guessed some bitterness of life
in hard-mouthed Sparta drove her queen of sexual
intelligence and beauty to make such a down-bound trip.
Then they simply could not rest
until they forced you back, stripped of your
protectors, stripped of your freedom, stripped
finally of your life. Just the day before
we Amazons arrived, they had killed Hector,
Troy's best warrior, next to me of course.

Helen

And who did you say you were?

Pen

Penthesilea, Amazon Queen, who went once
to war to save Queen Helen (that was you).
"Able to make men mourn" my name signifies,
supreme Amazon speeding to the neediness of Troy,
leader of twelve good warrior maidens,
battle-scarred
and with fierce reputation. We were the last
hope that queenly Troy could keep intact
and reachable, the greatest beauty in the world.

> *(Crows begin entering one by one; they lounge
> around the bar casually; then as Pen and Helen
> speak they act out battle scenes; they are Amazon
> Warriors though some take the parts of male
> Greek warriors in the fray.)*

Helen
    I remember that day.
    The sky was a sheet of crystal
    and the wind was still.
    I ran to see your arrival
    from my windowsill.
    You were like Artemis to us,
    you arrow-carrying bear-dikes.
    I could tell how Hector
    and the other men had learnt
    some of their skill from you,
    and then too, what can confuse
    a man more than a naked female
    breast with a bloody ax behind it?

Pen
    You and I met before the fight.
    I rode into the hall
    on the great long-legged stride
    my mother prized me for.

    You turned almost at once
    to look me up and down.
    My cheeks burned with pride
    though inside
    I felt more like a clown.

Helen
    The Amazons were coming!
    To fight on our side!
    We women were electrified.
    You looked strange to us
    but exhilarating.
    I was especially electrified
    by you.

Pen
    I knew it too, that moment
    at least, when our eyes met across the room.
    I was your last battle ax
    and you threw it.

Helen

    By then, with the war in its tenth year,
    I don't think I cared much
    whether I stayed with Paris
    or my husband won and took me home.
    You put up the hardest fight they ever saw,
    carved their gullets and split their craws,
    set them mewling in their own fear,
    pinned to the ground with their own spears.
    I had never seen men die of terror.

Pen

    You flew into a cloud of dust, Helen,
    you withdrew.
    We didn't know what slavery of your beauty
    stood on the other side
    of my downfall.

Helen

    I remember that day.
    During the fight
    some of us thought
    we should run outside
    to help you, stand beside
    with shield and mace and other weapons.
    Someone reminded us,
    you trained all your life
    for this—we are different,
    built to carry a different burden,
    stand in a different place.

Pen

    I don't know how you are or are not built.
    I know you were watching
    when Achilles killed me.
    I know it affected you horribly.

Helen

    I wanted to turn my face
    and couldn't.

I was transfixed.
No one imagined
you could ever be beaten,
let alone raped
and dragged around like a dishrag.
Everything fractured then
as the sword clubbed and then went in,
not just the ribs and skull,
the full picture
went to pieces, I saw the
world break like a dropped egg.

Pen

Helen your beauty
and your godlike features
cracked like shell
after my own cracking face
and graceless fall.
Oh god Helen, we lost the war;
we lost each other in the war.
I was your tooth
and they pulled it
I was your dagger
and they tore it
from your hand.

Amazon Chorus

She was your voice
and they slit your throat;
she was your breath
caught like a duck in a gill net.

Helen

I stood with all
the women on the wall, watching,
hands clutching
as you lay on the sand
blood-drained and stiffening.

Pen

> I was your arrow
> against the foe
> I was your backbone
> bent low
> oh lady of sorrow
> I was your bow.

Amazon Chorus

> Helen, your arrow—
> where is it?
> Is it hidden
> in your pocket?
> Is it long like a rocket,
> or is it round as a locket?
> Is it a bee sting?
> Is it stored in a quiver,
> or under your disgust for slimy things?
> Helen—your arrow,
> do you have it?

Helen

> How horrible that this happened to you,
> how horrible what they did to you.

Pen

> They did it to you, too.
> We have to move through memory
> as the wind sifts through dust, examining
> everything for clues.
> My corpse self was crow-eaten
> and discarded, my power stolen.
> I have to move through that scene
> to another, to the dream remembered,
> a dream of wild horses
> of women's fingers tangled in the manes,
> and tangled with each other,
> in a dream of what we do with horses

when we do it all together,
when we do it with one motive.   ‡

Helen

Oh yes, I'd rather talk of horses.
At home I have a shelf of lovely glass horses.
And I've heard of Amazons with horses.
I've heard you do the most
amazing things with horses.

Amazon

Horse my pelvis, horse my thighs,
horse the thunder in my eyes . . .

Helen

What *do* you do with horses?

Amazon Chorus

As for what we do with horses   †
it's none of your business,
it's none of your knowing
what rides we mounted
what circles rode, what songs shouted.

It's not for your understanding
what fires we kindled
in autumn darkness,
what flames we handled
when the moon was
breathless.
                    As for what
we did in tandem
it was the bonding of warriors,
as for what we did of ritual
it was what you now call: actual.

As for what we learned in shadows
it's not of your fathom,
it's deep as molasses
or a parade of motorcycles,

it's the well-waxed chassis
with eighty horsepower
and electromagnetic fuel injection.

As for what we do with horses
we ride them like forces,
as for what we do with forces,
we tug them in closer.
As for what we do with borders
we cross and uncross them,
as for what we do with curses,
we put them in purses
and fling them to blazes.

As for what we do with horses
we fondle their noses
we drape them in roses
and race them on courses,
it's a great-hearted outpouring
with the whole crowd cheering,
it's not for the artless,
it's the marriage of speed,
the finest run on the finest steed,
it's what we whisper in their ears,
it's how their hoofbeats whisper up
to us, "Destiny, destiny, destiny . . .
rides on opportunity."
It's the brave heart churning,
to nearly bursting,
it's the pent blood pressing
the hot breath
to the hotter neck,
it's the hand slapping and the wet flank
slapping back against the hand,
as for what we do with horses,
it's the rush of our great trying,
it's the tension of our lunging
it's the love of promising
it's the flesh imagining itself flying

it's the flash of light before thundering,
it's the dark ring of opening,
it's the way we have of living
in the dust of the wind.   ‡

Helen

That's not anything I've ever done with horses.

Pen

After the fall of women's power,   †
in the dust whirl of dream
I lay for centuries hardly moving,
paralyzed,
recalling only the last act, the rape
that Achilles bent to vent himself on me.
I thought I would never be free of it,
until at last I began to live again,
and again, to hang at the corner of the ceiling
and recall who I had been.
I saw myself a Roman soldier
on the march,
saw myself a Viking on the Normandy coast,
I saw myself a tender-hearted soldier
in the First World War.
Saw myself at last reborn
in my own killer's form.

Helen

You have lived over and over
in the bodies of men?

Pen

When he took our Amazon strength
to be his own he became a soldier; women
such as you and I hung high on a peg, burning.

Helen

Like Joan of Arc! Hung on a stake!

Pen

Yes, high on a peg, and then down
to the scorpion ground. I have been down

to the bottom of the ditch;
I have been down overcome by my own corpse-stench.
If you could just join forces with me now
you would find the awesome power of nothing
you've been looking for.

Helen

I don't want awesome nothing
and I don't want dust,
I certainly can't join forces
with you, I'm not
part of your war.

Pen

My war?

Helen

I stood apart from everyone,
I stood on the ramparts of the wall,
while men on the inside warred
with men on the outside,
and you manlike Amazons
mixed it up with the worst of them.
I stood on the wall; I fled on the stair;
I was hardly there at all.
I hid out in Egypt,
keeping the occult sciences that once
belonged to me;[1] I have no part of war.
I live in a glass house, with glass horses;
I hardly ever come face to face with my own forces.

Amazon Chorus

Helen, the nature of your strength,
what is it?

Helen

Everything I have or am
I give to men now,
they fought and won it,
isn't that correct?
Besides they are so strong,

and losers mushy-chested
and contemptible.

Amazon Chorus
Strong, there are so many kinds
of strong.
Men are steadfast
in what they want,
that is one.
Amazon strength
lives in the wind,
in a dust-particle dance of transformation.

Helen
And Helen's strength, what is it?
Is it the strength of love?

Amazon Chorus
Helen, your strength
is in your memory.

Helen
And is my memory my mother?
What are my memories?

Amazon Chorus
Memory is the mother of truth;
and truth is the mother of beauty;
and beauty is the real mother
of real science.

Pen
Helen. I was your tooth,
and it rotted.
I was your knife and you dropped it
from your hand.
I have endured every humiliation of the battle-lost,
the war-torn. I have sometimes wished not to be born.
I have been called every vile name,
and worst of all, you have seen,
and feared, and scorned, and shunned me.
But names are only identity games, and suffering ends

in toughness or death, what I have never been
is a slave, only the side that lost the war.
Yet without me as the dagger by your side,
slave is quite a bit of what you are.

Helen

Oh you go on so long,
and you're so wrong.
I'm not a slave—
I'm just well-behaved.
I live in a nice glass house
with glass bells—
I've been a cherished, petted child—
lucky person, lucky life—

Amazon Chorus

Helen, your horses,
what are they?
Can you ride them
or do you hide them?
Are they broken?
Do you deny them,
can you even find them?
Helen—your horses,
do they lead you,
or follow?
Are you keeping them,
in what meadow?

Pen

My memory is a long one,
it gives me no rest.
Though you recoil from me now
dressed in my blood and dirt,
and with my wounded breast—
is my sack of being
too leaky for your good taste?
Still, I'll give you advice
and of what I have—the best . . .

You say you stand
on the wall, apart, yet
everywhere there's a war
there you are, beautiful, desired
and right in the middle of it.
So I know you're a player,
whether or not you admit it.
This is what I know, Helen,
of the nature of war,
if you stay in battle long enough
you'll find you carry every arm,
do every harm
in every heart
of every storm.
No horse you own remains unridden,
no hand you hold remains unplayed.

Helen

And what of love in all this talk of death?
And what of my high hopes?
And my force? What is it? Is it politics?
Is it science?
What is it really can rise from dust?

Amazons

Helen, your forces
are in the beauty of your memory,
do you remember?
Can you ride them like horses?

Helen

What is my science?

Amazons

Your science is in the memory of your beauty.

Helen

How can I re-form from simple dust
to remember myself, how can I ever understand
the nature of my beauty?

Amazon Chorus

    Under the mask of Helen smiling
    lies the Foe,
    under the mask of the Foe
    lies a dead Amazon,
    under the mask of the fallen Amazon
    lies Helen, sleeping.
    Under the mask of Helen sleeping
    lies the lady of the underworld
    birthing fury,
    and under the fury
    stands the bull god,
    wild-eyed, waiting
    for his sacrifice.

Helen

    I remember, I remember, I remember—
    the sky *is* a sheet of crystal on a day like this—
    and I remember the whole war now,
    and later my own crashing fall
    and loss of power.
    What a splash I made!
    Golden light went everywhere,
    a sparkling cloud of dust.
    No wonder they call it Fairy dust!
    What powers I had! What sciences!
    Healing—predicting, even controlling weather.
    Yet after that war
    I was no longer one superior
    focal point of light, like Venus.
    I was scattered everywhere, wind-torn,
    my villages burned to underground,
    the old folks going down
    on the forced marches,
    after the teachers and the intellectuals
    spewed their own blood along the fences,
    while the women huddled in whore camps
    with their brains stripped out of their skulls,

and everyone ate napalm rations,
our young men being clubbed to death in
the police stations, our children turned to strangers
in the boarding schools of force-fed reculturation,
after he sent the smallpox-saturated blankets,
after he marched my babies to the jailing baby school,
after the bombs, after the secret warehouse torture,
after the famine and the relocation,
after the war . . .

Pen

I became your fallen warrior eating dust,
my lips flattened in it,
while dogs pissed
on my torn coat the way a man, a soldier
might rape my
corpse between the legs, and call it
love or lust or even by its better name,
conquest, trying to do the sorcery of
soul-theft.

Helen

I became a cloud, forgetful,
fearful and unpredictable.
Now how can I ever gather myself together again?
Are you one of my forces?
And you—who are *you?*
You're more blown apart
than I am. I expected a glorious
Amazon, not a blood-dripping corpse.

Pen (kneeling)

Oh I know I offend you
with my leaking chest
and bitter mouth,
my messages of hard reality,
but Helen, reach to touch me,
touch my fingers—dust we always have
to turn to;

touch is all we have to give
each other, while we're here.

Tangle fingers with me now
so you can remember who you are,
and I can live on earth again.

> *(They touch fingers; Helen wipes hers on her shirt.)*

Helen (thoughtfully)
Now another woman's blood is on my hands.   ↓

> *(Pen suddenly laughs, though not derisively and
> not at Helen, pulling off her mask to reveal herself
> as Ereshkigal. She stamps her foot, and all the
> Amazons become Crows who stamp their feet,
> too, and howl and whoop. Helen recoils.)*

SCENE TWO: ABOVEWORLD

Her Shadow Falls Across Me

*The basement of a large industrial building, preferably a steam plant,
with lots of pipes, clouds of white steam, and some rubber plants.
ENKI is alone, dressed as an engineer, humming to himself, making
adjustments. He addresses the audience in his first speech.*

Enki (in greasy overalls and with wrench in hand)
Thoughts are public things,
ever think such a quaint idea?
(You got it from me, naturally.)

Have you thought about thoughts?
Do you have some?
Where do you think they come from?

Thoughts are points of sound/light   †
sheathing
stratospheres.
From up there
I have watched human beings
thinking they think.
Really, they hear.
Tuned in to radio bands
of collective understandings,
flashes of insight
going inside from outside.
Once in a while
a group magnetizes
a thought form, called
"a new idea," a sound mote—
and blaring it out
gets it caught up there in the sheath
with a new specific ionic band
all its own.
From above, this event appears
as a point of lighter air
rising into the biosphere.
Caught up there, it's available
to anyone else who wishes to share,
and to think they thought
by shifting their inner ears
to the exact note, and tuning in.
Interesting idea, this
that I thought I heard
while I was there.   ·   ↓

Now I'm here, below below,
doing weekend duty
and fix-'em-ups.

Nin (entering)
   I've been to the Father gods of Destiny,   †
   War, and Economic Effort, talked to Proud Thomas

with his new girlfriend—the faithless husband!—
to see if any would help fair Helen.
To a man they were against it.
"We told her so! We told her so!"
they cry as though to add prediction
to their list of skills in lying.
I'm the only one who's caring for her person.
"Don't let her priceless, magnificent being
be broken in the underworld,"
I call to them, "don't let your forest be
a slag heap, or your river run with photographic fluid.
Don't let the daughter of beauty walk the streets
with rotten teeth and broken face."
I begged, I railed.
"What if she were your daughter, would
you leave her to disease and pimps and beggars,
drunkards and thieves and junkies,
and the irresponsible greed
of international companies?"
To no avail, they turn away.
"She wanted everything, to be a wife and mother
and a woman of the world. Let her see the price
she has to pay," they say. Their jealousy is evident.
Now I have come to make one final appeal to Enki,
last god on my list, the wisdom of nature,
a god whose peculiarities are entirely his.   ⌇

Enki

Who calls my name?

Nin

I looked everywhere for you   †
and couldn't find you
in your usual haunts where I would expect
the god of natural things to be.
You weren't at Brighton-by-the Sea,
or the Black Forest, the Amazon River, or at Grand Teton.
I cabled Tibet, even spoke to the folk
who know the Glacier Elk,

tried all the deserts and the water tables,
checked out your favorite mountain peaks.
Your whereabouts were a mystery to monks,
physicists, the Audubon Society,
the Sierra Club, *and* Greenpeace.
Finally I consulted my Tarot
and was sent here—to below
this great metropolis of human activity.
What is it you are doing here, down under a city?   ⸸

Enki

Oh I have to be the one to help it go.
See that sign above my office door:
"GE," that's me—Grand Engineer.   †
You know, they think they move
in opposition to me—
they're so much closer to me
than they know.
If I don't show up
on weekends at least
they blow up all the circuits
on their circuit boards, the bakers
can't control the yeast,
the airwaves jam, chemical combinations
simply don't combust,
and the sewage backs up the sluice
to swamp them. I just make sure the electric juice
remembers which way it needs to flow
so the city has its power, perhaps also
a little golden beauty and a bit of grace.
It's my way of keeping faith
between the human beings and me.   ⸸

Nin

Speaking of things golden and beautiful,
I don't come for myself but rather to appeal
to you for Helen's sake.
Her grace and beauty strip away in an underground
cave of rare adventure. It's all very well

for her to learn some new and rougher ways of being,
but to stay forever—
where the rats dwell—
that's hell.
To stay forever in some gross industrial cave, that's
a kind of narcosis from which, to keep her beauty
active in our lives—we all must wake—

Enki

Why do you make such effort for another woman,
for Helen? For someone fallen—
are you in love with her?

Nin

I don't know my motive or my gain,   †
I know her shadow falls across me
where I lay.

I know we must have been close
since now she's gone
I walk my life a ghost.

I don't know our middle or our end.
I know in our beginning
we were friends.

I don't understand her motive or her gain,
I don't know where she's been
or where she'll be again.

I know my life is not the same
without her flamboyance, or her flame,
I know her shadow falls across me where I lay.

I know I must be feeling bad
since now when I sleep
it's underneath my bed.

I never undertook to know her mind,
I'll never know her motive
or her plan.

I know her shadow falls across me
where I stand—   ↓

Enki

    Good gracious, don't go on.
    I can see this has you very down,
    though I think you know more about her future
    than you're letting on,
    and yes of course I'll help,
    what else does nature do but try to help.
    I'm amiable, mostly, both for building up and
    tearing down. You want apples, ask the apple tree:
    rounder, redder, more juice. She'll comply
    as best she can. You want bombs that bomb the living
        substance
    out of all Bombay and any other place you
    care to name—well, you've got them.
    We try harder, faster, longer,
    here in nature land. I'll do what I can.
    Besides, I certainly could use some assistance
    teaching natural principles to the humans,
    they're so certain of their own unnaturalness
    they've made a cult of being ugly.

Nin

    Ugly is incomplete beauty in my view.
    Beauty caught short before it can complete
    the act to some full end.

Enki

    No, ugly's a thing of its own,
    a use of pain and alienation
    toward some slavish end.
    Those who believe they are ugly
    objectify the rest of us.

Nin

    But is it natural then?

Enki

    Oh it's natural enough,
    but you don't have to live your days
    in the very gut of Nature—you can, in your life,
    choose qualities . . .

Nin

    What is it you suppose our Helen needs
    to get her freed?

Enki

    Someone like you, I think, a friend!
    Someone to stand beside
    without judgment, and to follow through.
    We can't send you, you have to stay above,
    and do your mourning of her loss.
    I'll have to make some friends to see her through.
    Marvelous objects come from dirt.
    I've plenty underneath my fingernails; don't look
    if creative process makes you squeamish.
    Where do jelly doughnuts come from, if not dirt?
    Just let me give them some interesting body shape
    to walk around in for a lifetime . . .
    These androgynous beings, genderless
    and all-engendered, fairies of light
    and liveliness. I call them into being purposefully,
    to help restore the god of beauty
    to our daily lives.

> *(Kur and Gal appear, stretching and waking; they*
> *are a young dike and a young faggot,[1] dressed in*
> *self-conscious country clothes such as clean new*
> *overalls, and with the appearance of*
> *health and innocence.)*

Enki

    May the fairies be vegetarian!   †
    May they be pure of heart as the earth is
    in her shirt of dirt.
    Let them be pure as air on Mount Olympus,
    air inside an Atlantic blowfish, air pumped
    into a rubber tire in 1932 in Nevada
    before the explosions, before Reno, before traffic
    smogged up Tahoe.
    Let them be pure of body, let them

be vegetarian! Fruitarian! Breatharian! Let them
eat only bean sprouts, and then
only by inhaling the delicate breath of
someone else who has eaten bean sprouts!
Let them eat only thoughts!
Let them tell only pristine lies.
Let them be pure of brain, let them read everything
and watch thousands of movies. Let them seldom
have contact of a dangerous sexual nature,
let them have lots of love but
let them do much of their mating
on the telephone. Let them not be lonely, and
if they have to be alone,
let them be alone together; let them care for each other.
And let them get past the gatekeeper of the deadly
underworld, cleverly disguised
as a clean lean cloud of lean clean flies!
Let them carry the water of life and the tree of life,
to keep the apple of love and beauty growing in their
    hearts.   ↯

Nin

Enki, I'm so glad I came to you,
a woman is rich whose friends are true.
Helen will be back among us soon,
spreading her good cheer
and healing our wounds.

Enki

I have some bottled, bubbly, crisp
imported water here
for them to take down to her
for her reconstitution,
and a gorgeous Payless Nursery
rubber plant.
And now we've got to figure out
how to trick the Vixen of the Great Below
before she reaches out to grab
these pristine creatures and then hangs them up

to roil and rot
before they get Queen Helen out.

> *(Enki pulls Nin and the two fairies into a circle of*
> *conspiracy, drawing on the floor with his wrench*
> *as they continue making plans.)*

GATE FIVE: BELOWWORLD

A Woman among Motorcycles

ERESHKIGAL'S *Crow Bar. The decor is greatly improved. It is Hal-*
loween, so there are black cats and pumpkins here and there. Most of
the CROW DIKES *are tattooed and dressed in black leather, carrying*
staffs or swords, with eyepatches and the like. Some are costumed as
bees or nurses. The crossed swords at the back of the bar have been
taken down and one is on the bar. HELEN *has tied the other to her*
broom and is hacking at one of the roof support poles, or perhaps
a large standing coatrack, then spears it through as though it were a
bull and she a matador. Between thrusts she drinks liquor from a glass;
there are several shot glasses near her and it is obvious she has drunk
quite a bit. She is looking disheveled and as though she is not taking
very good care of herself. ERESHKIGAL *is counting money out of the*
register or taking inventory. NOTHING *is tending bar.*

Helen (grunting and growling with effort, teeth clenched, ramming the
pole with the sword or spear)
   Now I've got you where I want you.
   You'll never escape my fury.

Crow
   What is Venus doing I wonder?

Crow
   She's doing some swordplay.

Crow
    She's handling a big pricking stick.

Crow
    That's cutting.

Crow
    It's CAW stick.

Crow
    She's practicing being a matador.

Crow
    She's spearing Taurus.

Crow
    She's trying to cut through all that bull.

                    *(Helen whirls with the spear, knocking a glass off
                        the table. It shatters, which infuriates her.)*

Ereshkigal
    I hope *we* manage to escape your fury.
    What is it you are doing? Is that your costume?
    What are you dressed up as, Ernest Hemingway?[1]

Helen (insulted)
    I'm trying to learn to be a warrior;
    I though that was what you wanted.

Ereshkigal (coming out from behind the bar)
    You don't have to learn to be a warrior.
    You have to remember having been one.

                                        (Helen tries to speak.)

Ereshkigal
    Silence, Inanna.
    When you have a memory, you shall speak.

                    *(She holds a full-sized hand mirror in front of
                    Helen's face; Helen takes it and gapes into it, trying
                    to smooth her hair and making tough faces.)*[2]

    Look, Helen, look into your mind!
    If yours is sodden, look into mine!

81

Women were warriors in Caesar's time!
Have you never remembered the warrior queens
who resisted conquest on Europe's greens?
Have you never remembered the bulldike queen
who nearly unseated the Roman's claim
on England, during Nero's reign? [3]

> *(Ereshkigal takes the mirror back, then goes to the
> pile of costumes, rummages through, and comes up
> with a red braided wig, a long spear, and a long
> robe or tunic, Celtic style, which she puts on. As
> she performs, the Crow Warrior dikes act out
> various parts while Helen clumsily but
> persistently joins in.)*

I, Boudica,   †

a queen am I,
a warrior and a shaman.
Shameless is my goddess and ferocious;
my god's foot cloven.

I am protectress of my horse-bound clansmen.
A red-haired, full-robed, bronze-belted swordswoman,
I am a queen of sacred groves and other old realms
where astronomers divine from droves of animals
or flocks of birds, and study the signs in palms;
a queen of times when men are lovers to the men
and the women to the women,
as is our honored pagan custom.
Ever and ever did we think to reign
in such an independent fashion,
until the day the foe came.

He came to my temple.
In ships he came to me.
Our possessions upon the prow of his ship he put.
He with hired soldiers came
to our self-ruled regions.
The foe, he with legions, entered my court.

He put his hands upon me, he filled me with fear.
My garments he tore away, and sent them to his wife.
The foe stripped off my jewels and put them on his son.
He seized my people's lands and gave them to his men.

He put his hands upon me, he filled me with rage.
I spoke to him in anger.
I told him of his danger.
So for me myself did he seek in the shrines.
In front of my folk he had me beat;
and this was not the worst I had to meet:
he seized my young daughters and had them raped.

He seized my daughters
and had them raped;
oh queen of heaven, queen
who shatters the mountains;
how long before you must my
face be cast in hate?

A queen am I, my cities have betrayed me.
A queen, Boudica, am I, my cities have betrayed me.
In that rebellious year
of sixty-one A.D. I rose up,
I, Boudica, over the countryside
from clan to clan and ear to ear,
I drove round in a chariot,
my daughters with me.

To every woman and every man
I spoke:
        "Now is the battle drawn
        which must be victory or death.
        For today I am more than your queen,
        and more than your mother deeply wronged,
        I am all the power of women brought down;
        one who will fight to reclaim her place.
        This is my resolve. Resolve is what I own.
        We women shall fight. The men can live,
        if they like, and be slaves."

And so we went to war.
Our men went with us.
And for centuries since, the foe has
searched for us in all our havens,
secret circles, rings and covens;
almost always we elude him,
we who remember who we are;
we who are never not at war.

On that day
didn't I, Boudica,
didn't I up rise,
didn't I slay,
didn't I hold fast
the ancient ways.

Wasn't I like a wall
wasn't I a great dike
against a giant spill,
that iron sea
of Roman pikes
that came to conquer Gaul.

Even if for one day
didn't the foe almost fall,
didn't his teeth gnash,
wasn't his bladder galled,
didn't the foe, even he,
know fear;
he feared me.

He feared me, then,
in his being
unable to fully win
unable to fully kill
the rebel things
my name means,
he fears still.

He fears me still,
for my shameless guise

and lesbian ways;
for undefeated eyes,
a warrior's spine
and all my memories
of women's time.

A queen am I, my city
needs to find me.
Meantime the foe arrives
unceasingly
from every steel-grey sea,
by every mountain road on earth
he enters all my cities
and for me myself he seeks
in my varied shrines,
in my temples he pursues me,
in my halls he terrifies me,
saying, "Cause her to go forth."
He goads. He burns, he murders.
He erodes.

A queen am I,
a warrior and a shaman.
Shameless is my goddess and ferocious;
my god's foot cloven.

A queen am I, a living memory
who knows her own worth
and who remembers that the future
is the past rehearsed,

and *not should I go forth*
unless it be for battle girthed.
Unless it be for battle girthed,
and belted, *not should I go forth*

until the foe is driven from the earth.[4]   ⸶

*(The Warrior Crow Dikes cheer wildly and toast their
queen, pulling out bottles and parading around in
their costumes.)*

Ereshkigal (breathless from her effort)
  Who else has a memory, let her speak.

> *(A Crow Dike steps forward, dressed like a Viking,*
> *with long blond braids and a sword; she is*
> *a large woman.)*

Crow Dike
  I am Ildreth remembering.[5]   †

  All in green I rode a tall horse
  deep in the North woods, my hair
  so yellow it was white and fine and
  down to here.

  Big as any conquering Viking man I tracked them
  and by trickery caught one or maybe two.
  Stepping noiseless behind I ran
  one fellow through
  before his ax could pop my skull.
  Blood along my scabbard told the others
  to steer clear.

  Protecting other women and the children
  and the older people was my task.
  Proof is here on my face, in this new mark . . .
  I studied in the mirror this morning
  getting ready for work . . .
  or was this from just last weekend
  when I, racing nowhere in my car,
  wrecked it, going head first
  through the windshield and being
  drunk when the cops came,
  got out, of course, and blindly fought them
  and was beat raw to the pulp
  that left, from cheek to jaw,
  this deep pink scar?

  I swear I'm going to quit this life
  of drinking whiskey, trying to keep
  a girlfriend—spending all my money
  in the bar.

I'm going up to the country to build a house
with my own hands,
find some ground—to love,
to leap, and land upon.

I'm going to the country to build a house,
maybe invite a few friends,
some strangers—people in my same bind,
no name for what they're doing in
their sacks of skin.
Going to go looking for my real mind,
the one I think I once had
before my memory got lost.
Going to sit at the back of my house
and gather my old thoughts
        like scattered birds,
and make images of mud,
and words and glass,
and gather my old gods
        like a flock of birds
from a soul-place,
and touch my fingers
gently to my own
and to my lover's face,
and study up.   ꜛ

Ereshkigal
Who else has a memory, let her speak.

> *(Helen steps into the semicircle. As she speaks, the
> Crow Dikes become men Motorcycle Crows, revving
> their engines as they circle her. Ereshkigal sits at
> the bar, watching.)*

Helen
I remember a time, a night when the sky
was a sheet of crystal and the air was dry,
I became a Woman in the Middle of Motorcycles.

One night, a night of the full moon   †
rising just as Venus lowered in the West,

I went out walking, miles
into the hills, alone,
not even my dog went with me.
It never occurred to me to carry a gun.
I crossed an abandoned parking lot
whose asphalt had begun to rot,
with grass and thistles already pushing
thinly through,
and the first roar of the motorcycle
only startled me,
then two more, then three,
I wasn't frightened until they were five
and circling me, their black boots
and jackets armor against the moonlight.
Dense with terror, I turned to see
they were ten, all single men, grinning
and grim and watching me.

I knew instinctively this was not the time to fall.
Begging, showing fear or pain would be my death.
I drew a great first breath
and throwing back my head, I called down the moon,
"Mother Moon," then
"Mother Venus," I called,
as the cycles crawled past, circling and waiting,
and roaring and watching me.
And then I said my mother's name
and hers and hers and hers and hers

Grandmother Mabel I said,
Grandmother Kate I said,
Grandmother Clementine I said,
Grandmother Mary I said,
then I called my aunts to me,
Margaret, who baked bread when grandpa died, Helen I
    know nothing
of at all, Agnes spanked me till I cried, Sybil helped build her
own cinderblock house by the shores of Lake Michigan,

Gertrude who wasn't mechanical drove her
very first car
straight up a telephone pole,
Betty worked forty years in a grocery store, and Blanche
wore a high-topped dress,
black stockings, and a brilliant smile
in the only photo I have seen,
when she was seventeen, in 1917.

When I had finished with my aunts,
I called the gods and mothers of the gods, Mary,
Anna, Isis, Ishtar, Artemis, Aphrodite, Hecate, Oyá, Demeter,
Freya, Kali, Kwan Yin, Pele, Yemanya, Maya, Diana, Hera,
     Oshun,
and after that some saints, Barbara, Joan, and Brigit;
as my memory ran out I made up some more saints,
canonized them on the spot.

And finally I called my friends including from high school,
Francine who has ESP and never leaves me,
Karen who wore black and was a warrior, Betty who is able to
live her dreams, Karen who wears pink sweaters and has a
     face of
sunshine, Alice of the little furry paws and dedicated life,
Carol piercingly faithful to her own axis, Pat whose heart is
always hanging in my hallway, careful careful careful Eloise,
Willyce with her singing voice, all the rest, then each woman I
have ever worked with, then some heroines, Eleanor, Gwen,
Gertrude, Margaret, Amelia, Hilda, till I had chanted every
woman's name I knew.

When I was through I said them all over again,
turning in my own circle with my face up and the moon
shining in, it must have been an hour or more I whirled
and chanted, filling my ears with my woman-naming roar.

When I opened my eyes
the angry men were gone;
Venus had set, the moon was down,

I stood in the asphalt field
alone—
and not at all alone.[6]   ↓

> *(As the above proceeds, the Motorcycle Crows one*
> *by one spin out of the circle and freeze in positions*
> *of goddess statues: sitting palms up on their knees,*
> *standing growling like shamanic Kali, standing*
> *gracefully with palms lifted like Kwan Yin or the*
> *Cretan snake goddess, standing with hands in*
> *Marian prayer attitude, standing aiming a bow*
> *and arrow like the warriors Diana or Oyá,*
> *arms clasping each other like the reunited*
> *Demeter and Persephone.)*

Ereshkigal
    I can see that you already see, Helen,
    there is more to standing
    than simply having standing, and more
    to understanding than simply falling down;

    there is standing your own ground.

> *(The Crow Warriors break their statue postures and*
> *begin dancing a ring dance, with Helen and*
> *Ereshkigal dancing too, Helen so drunk she is*
> *staggering in and out of sync. Stage rear Nothing*
> *also dances, alone and spinning in*
> *the opposite direction.)*

GATE SIX: BELOWWORLD

Judgment of Helen

ERESHKIGAL*'s Crow Bar, with* ERESHKIGAL, HELEN, NOTHING, *and*
CROW DIKE JUDGES. *The bar is now completely spruced up, looking*
colorful and light, with candles and green decorations. There is a lot

of crystal in evidence, as well as ERESHKIGAL's *wind chimes. But* HELEN *is looking terrible, haggard and doped up, dirty and disheveled, with dark circles under her eyes. She is drinking at the upstage center table, and there are pill bottles and other paraphernalia of drug addiction on the table also, or any other contemporary signs of deterioration. She is laughing and talking very closely, perhaps dancing with* NOTHING, *her voice noticeably high-pitched and tense. The* CROWS, *who are* JUDGES *in black gowns in this Gate, are playing pool.*

Crows (singing)
    Green, green, green is the color
    of my true love's hair,
    and of her teeth, and of her toes,
    and of her face so fair.

Ereshkigal (striking the wind chimes)
    Deny, deny, deny, deny.
    Seven venial virtues
    cloud the crystal of her eye.

    She's keeping counsel with Nothing;
    I keep the counsel of the carrion crow.

    As hour by hour, I go on growing older   †
    I like the carrion crow
    as my advisor.
    Not many are more wicked, not many are wiser.

    For advisor I'll take the carrion crow
    to stand upon my shoulder
    with his caw-caw-coffin chatter
    keeping me self-conscious.

    Keeping me so super conscious
    that my flesh, however pretty
    and however dear to me
    belongs to someone else tomorrow
    (or to no one)
    and is only borrowed clay.

Is only modeled clay, my loves,
to animate the fray
and we'll slough it off to burrow
in a lighter cloth of sky.

In a lighter coat of sky, my bird,
to lay out the next play,
we'll cough it off to burrow
in the beauty of the sky.

As for beauty of the being,
it isn't fixed in time
longer than the ching ching ching
of a wind chime.

It's an animating play, my crow,
of light on surfaces.
Like the carrion bird I carry
on my shoulder, beauty strips away
the dross, so we can fly—

in a lighter coat of sky, my friend,
in a wind chime's clime—
and we'll laugh it off to burrow
in a lighter cloth of time.   ‡

Helen (her voice heavy with cynicism and disillusion)
If the mother of life is death
who is the mother of death?

Crow Chorus of Judges (rapid exchange)

Crow
There's no crow like an old crow.   †

Crows
CAW CAW CAW

Crow
What has a crusty shell
and turns red when it is boiling mad?

Crow
A crow dad!

92

Crows
CAW CAW CAW

Crow
What gets all decked out
and then hangs from a peg
in order to frighten people like us?

Crow
A scarecrow! [1]

Crows
CAW CAW CAW

Crow
Darken up, you crows!
We're here to seriously, or is it cereally, or is it
surlily, or is it surely or is it sorely or is it
scornfully or is it scorefilly—

Crow
We're here to CAWnsider—

Crows
CAW CAW CAW

Crow
Here to CAWnsider the CAWS of death—

Crow
And to try the goddess of life and beauty—

Crow
Try life!

Crow
Give life a trial!

Crow
CAWL life to the stand!

Crow
Bring out the evidence—

Crow
The evidence is here in the form of this lovely lady.

Helen (self-mockingly)
   I am the planet Venus, traveling toward the dawn—

Crow
   Who thinks she is Venus incarnate—

Crow
   Evidently—

Crow
   The evidence is evident—

Crow
   Die, you Helen—

Crow
   The first CAWS of death is this:
   first, it was alive,
   then, it died;
   therefore my CAWnsidered opinion is:

Crows
   CAW CAW CAW

Crow
   The CAWS of death is life—

Crow
   A scandalous revelation—

Crow
   Yet imminently true—

Crow
   And effectively false—

Crow
   It is true
   everything that is now dead
   was formerly alive
   and if *A* inevitably precedes *B*
   we are obviously talking CAWsation—

Crow
   And CAWruption.

Crow
> And CAWnsternation.

Crow
> Therefore, in retaliation
> I CAWndemn life to death.

Two Crows
> Brilliant! Charming! Correctly morbid!
> Essential logic!

Crows
> CAW CAW CAW

Crow
> Therefore I CAWndemn all life to death
> on the grounds that life is the CAWS of dying.

Crows
> CAW CAW CAW

Crow
> What grounds is this?

Crow
> CAWfee grounds—

Crows
> CAW CAW CAW

Crow
> Here it turns out that all this time
> dirty old Life is the primary CAWS of death—

Crow
> And must be punished—

Crows
> CAW CAW CAW

Crow
> Ooh oooh oooooh PUNished—

Crow
> How dreadful—

Crow
> I *hate* puns—

Crow
> How ungrateful—

Crow
> The Gateful Dread—

Crow
> A pun is the lowest form of twit—

Crow
> All life is hereby condamned to death—

Crow
> Condomed to which?

Crow
> A condomnation of death to life—

Crow
> I haven't felt so completely dead in a long time—

Crow
> You always did make me feel so dead—

Crow
> Let's go out on the town and die a little—

Crow
> Die it up while you can—

Crow
> It makes a person happy just to be so dead—

Crow
> Just to be so dead and a player in death's little game—

Crow
> Death's CAWn game—

Crows
> CAW CAW CAW

Crow
> It makes a person happy

just to be so depressed
and playing in the CAWn game of death—

Crows
CAW CAW CAW   ↓

Ereshkigal
Admit. Admit. Admit. Admit
when you see with the crystal eye of death
you'll see into the heart of it.
Here Helen, take this gift—a mirror
of memory.
This mirror is called,
"when this you see remember me." [2]
When your ordinary mind is cloudy,
look into this larger one.

Helen (taking the hand-mirror)
Oh Ereshkigal,
I'm not sure I want to see what's in here.
Oh god, I'm wrinkled around my eyes,
my mouth is puckered and my nose is misshapen.

Ereshkigal
Is that my face or yours that you see in there?
How is she ever going to look into her mind
when she can't see past her face?

Helen
Thomas was right.
Nothing ages a person like experience.

Nothing
I do the best I can.

Ereshkigal
Well, you're on your way to being a goddess,
of sagacity, at least, if not of popularity.
There are four kinds of memory;
you've recollected three. First, your mythic memory
as a goddess; second, your past-life history,
both the outer and inner versions in your mind;

third, the collective, consciously connected
recollections of your kind.
The last is of your own person,
the carefully buried splinter memories of childhood.
It's time for you to see whatever you dare to see.

Helen (staring past the mirror)
Mirror, mirror here I stand.
Help me remember who I am.

I was a cherished, petted child.

Ereshkigal (rolling her eyes)
Mirror, mirror in the sky.
Help her learn how not to lie.

Helen, your memory—   †
what is it?
Is it your mother?
Is it what she doesn't say?
Are there relatives you love
but never want to see?
Is it an evil glitter
in your own eye?

Is it the First Word,
or a dancing bird? Is it Idea
or is it a girl named Ida?
Or is it "I did it"?
Is it a story with an end and a beginning,
or a spider spinning her web
in every direction?
Is it space-time as an abstraction,
or is she a person?
Helen, your memory,
is it convection
or simple conviction,
is it a movie
or is it moving?
Helen, your memory! Look into your mind!   ‡
If yours is cloudy, then look into mine!

You were not only a petted, cherished child!
You were a martyr in your childhood time!

> *(Helen looks into the mirror and slowly and carefully*
> *begins to recover her childhood memories; she does*
> *not act drunk during this scene. She sometimes*
> *stands still, sometimes walks around the stage,*
> *holding her face, or pulling her hair, falling on*
> *Ereshkigal's shoulder to moan or cry. Ereshkigal is*
> *extremely tender and comforting.)*

Helen (shuddering)
　　The mind is a sheet of crystal
　　when your memory is clear.
　　I remember my fear.
　　I remember the entire war.
　　I remember being there.

　　My father struck me with his hand　　　　　　†
　　when I was five.
　　Lucky me, lucky me,
　　lucky to be alive.

　　My mother threw an iron at me
　　when I was four.
　　I lay unconscious on the
　　bathroom floor.

　　I don't know their motives
　　or their pain.
　　I know their shadows fell across me
　　where I lay.

　　My brother stabbed his sex in me
　　when I was three.
　　My anger dangles in my throat,
　　shamefully.

　　My sister pressed pillows on
　　my face at two.
　　Thick mush: To hush, to hush, I
　　struggle through.

I don't know the motives
of their rage.
I know their shadows fall across me
all my days.

My mother thrust a pin in me
when I was one.
Distrust. Distrust of
everyone.

I was a cherished,
petted child.
Lucky me, lucky me,
lucky to be alive.

Ereshkigal
Well done, you counted down to one.
But you aren't done.
Can you count down to zero
is the question.

Helen (after a long pause)
At zero I begin to understand
murders repeated, in my hand.
At zero I begin to count again:
my mother and I are one,

my father and I are two,
my brother and I are three,
my sister and I are four,
and my daughter she is five.

Sometimes she is cherished,
sometimes she is a battered child.
Lucky her, lucky her,
lucky to be alive.[3]   ┼

Ereshkigal (rocks Helen in her arms for a few moments, then she disengages from Helen, moving behind the bar)
Admit. Admit. Admit. Admit.   †
The eye of death
is at the heart of it,

and the clearest eye
is the eye of I-did-almost-die.
Admit. Admit. Admit. Admit.   ⸕

Helen
    Offer me something, Nothing.

Nothing
    I've offered you everything I have   †
    left in my bag:
    Have a depression, have two.
    Have a serious bout with the six-month flu.
    Have an addiction on repeated prescriptions,
    and have a habit of drink, of course.
    Have any addiction that devours
    your resources and sours your friendships.
    I'm really not particular;
    have whatever hurts you more, more, more.   ⸕

Ereshkigal (to Helen)
    I have to congratulate you   †
    for accepting everything Nothing
    has had to offer, all the liquor
    you could drink, every kind of drug
    to hallucinate you into every phony mental state,
    depression so steep your grave is half a kilometer deep,
    annihilation in all its clever shapes,
    alienation, nihilism, extreme materialism,
    projection, violent subjugation—
    repression, psychic and physical sterilization . . .
    congratulations to you for accepting
    all that was offered, including the most extreme
    isolation of any creature on or underneath
    this earth. It's not as simple as it may seem
    to poison the apple of self-esteem.
    Goody goody goody you,
    you gobbled the entire apple down,[4]
    and while you'll never be
    as big a Nothing

as you think you are, still you've done it all
at Nothing's beck and call,
and I congratulate you
for being such a nice girl, for taking it
without too much complaint,
for eating absolutely everything you found on your plate.   ✢

> *(During the following poem and chorus Helen*
> *drinks, takes drugs, sobs in desolation, passes out*
> *on the table, then drops to the floor in a*
> *state like death.)*

Helen

Is this what dying is really like?   †
I have the sensation of needing to regulate
my every breath;
of my life being something I stand and watch,
a falling star against a falling sky—
reality I thought I had in hand
suddenly dropping down
a funnel of air—
I have the sensation
of the black hole of creation
squeezing me through its bloody gate,
to what's out there;
what's out there?

I wait. I cannot breathe. I shake.
What if I admit, admit, admit,
and still can't make sense
of any of it?
What if I'm crazy?
What if I never again act right?
What if everything—
even the mirror of sound and sight—
is a lie?
What if all I ever do is die?
What if I don't, and hate
every minute of staying alive?
Is this what being born is like?   ✢

Crow
> The Queen of Swords will take you through
> the House of Horrors.   †

Crow
> Where is Helen now?

Crow
> She's gone to the House of Horse.

Crow
> She's gone to the House of Horus.[5]

Crow
> Horace took her to his house.

Crow
> She's gone over to the Horace House.

Crow
> Helen is a fallen woman.

Crow
> Falling through a crack.

Crow
> She's descending.

Crow
> Down goes our Venus.

Crow
> She's gone to Horrid Horace's Whorehouse.

Crow
> As a customer (or consumer I mean)?

Crow
> Not as a consumer, as one of the commodities.

Crow
> How venial.

Crow
> Falling onto her back.

Crow
> How funereal.

Crow

Falling onto her head.

Crow

How venerable.

Crow

Falling into her heart.

Crow

How vulnerable.

Crow

Falling into her vulgar vulva.

Crow

How venereal.

Crows	*Crow*
How venereal	an episode
How venereal	an afternoon
How venereal	a painting
How venereal	two flowers
How venereal	lady day
How venereal	mashed potatoes
How venereal	my life story
How venereal	love is the answer
How venereal	without trying
How venereal	dear old Mom
How venereal	a funeral
How venereal	someone's ambition
How venereal	as the world whirls
How venereal	at a snail's pace
How venereal	with Horace
How venereal	and how responsible
How venereal	and candied apples
How venereal	a corporation
How venereal	and how pig-headed

↓

*(The Crows lift Helen's limp body as they perform
this last chant, carry her to the crossbeam upstage
center, or to a large standing coatrack, or to a deeper*

*chamber and hang her on the back of a door by the
back of her dress or shirt. She hangs limp, facing
the audience, nearly over Ereshkigal's head.)*

Ereshkigal (to Helen)
    Helen, your memory! Look into your mind!
    If yours is sleeping, then look into mine!

(To audience.)

The secret is, love is all   †
we ever need to eat.
It's the vital golden flow
we get from wheat and meat and beets,
and art, and sex, and lovely conversation.

It's the glow that pours through doors
of any open-hearted person,
who if she doesn't know the secret,
doesn't keep it under lock and key,
leaks more for me, more for me.

I've taken all her offers,
to breach her coffers;
I've used her vitality
for my own young glow.

I have eaten her energy,
I have borrowed her beauty,
and I've gotten her to eat enough crow
to keep her forever here below.[6]   ‡

*(Ereshkigal holds her stomach and rocks in pain
and obvious sorrow.)*

GATE SEVEN: BELOWWORLD

Reconstitution: Just Stand Her Up Again

ERESHKIGAL's *Crow Bar has not changed since Gate Six except that the dead* HELEN *has been laid out on the bar. She is covered with a sheet of clear plastic.*[1] *Three days and nights have passed; the* CROW DIKES *have been holding a wake for her. The* CROWS *become* DE- MONS *near the end of this Gate, perhaps with widely banded black and yellow sweatshirts and pointed hats, long black fingernails, black and yellow stockings. At opening* ERESHKIGAL *is in pain, upstage left center, holding her stomach and chest, rocking back and forth. Mythically speaking, she is now giving birth to the new Inanna.*

Ereshkigal
>For three days and three nights
>she has looked like this.
>
>She lives on a glass mountain.   †
>She sleeps in a fishbowl.
>She's wrapped in Saranwrap.
>She's silent under her bell jar.
>She's locked in her tower of glass.
>
>She's Queen of the Ice Queens.
>She feels none of her feelings.
>She acts none of her actions.
>She speaks none of her insights.
>She hears only the crash
>of her own cold pulse,
>and the words: it's getting worse
>and worse
>and worse.   ‡

Crow
>She's inside Mount Venus.

Crow
>She looks terrible.

Crow
>She's dead.

Crow
>She looks dead.

Crow
>She smells dead.

Crow
>Whatever it was she did she overdid it.

Crow
>There's Nothing growing on her.

Nothing
>I'm not growing on her.
>She doesn't care for me.
>Leave me out of this.

>>>>*(Enter the Fairies, Kur and Gal. They are vivacious, dancing and chanting with tambourines. They commiserate with Ereshkigal in her mourning.)*

Fairies
>Isis, Inanna, Artemis, Kali,
>Ishtar, Gaia, Hera, Hecate.
>Lady of many lives we love you.
>Lady of deadly powers we need you.
>Lady of shadow motives we respect you.
>Lady of midnight skies we greet you.

>Are you sad?
>We're sad too.
>Does your heart ache?
>Our heart aches too.
>Does your womb hurt?
>Our womb hurts too.

Ereshkigal (interrupting)
>Alright, alright, GodDAMMit
>Now you've got me crying.
>What is it you want?
>I'll give it to you.

> Just don't try to flatter me.
> Offer them something, Nothing.

Fairies

> OH NO, anything else, but
> Nothing for us, no, Nothing for us.

Crow

> They don't want Nothing.

Fairies

> We're happy just as we are.[2]
> We've come to reconstitute the Queen.

Ereshkigal (pointing to Helen)

> That ugly thing?
> She's an Ice Queen.
> Unresponsive and cold,
> and growing old.

Crow

> She's an Ice Queen Crone.

(The Crows examine the Fairies)

Crow

> They've come to reconstitute her.

Crow

> To reconstitute her—

Crow

> —just stand her up again.

Crow

> To reconstitute her—

Crow

> —just add water.

Crow

> Stir a little—

Crow

> —just add lettuce.

Crow
Just add vitamins.

Crow
Just add a little music.

Crows
Just add Fairy dust!
Just add a little plasma!
Just add some rubber tubing!
Just plug something into her!

Crow
Just add some chloroform.

Fairies
Not chloroform—chlorophyll!

> *(The Fairies reconstitute Helen by changing her*
> *makeup and her clothes; meanwhile the Crow*
> *Dikes become Crow Demons.)*

Ereshkigal (still mourning Helen)
Control, control, control, control.   †
Seven venial virtues
cloud the crystal of her soul.
She came here believing she's something
and that though others are poor and downtrodden
she herself is wealthy and generous,
when Nothing is what she is related to.

She came here believing that nature loves her
and that mankind is a vicious brute.

She came here believing that while others rape
and batter and make war
she herself is innocent.

She came believing women are weak
and cannot defend themselves.

She came believing that she was a pampered,
petted child, never abused by her family.

Worst of all she came here believing her beauty
lives only in the vitality of her youth.
Since I have stolen her beauty,
she has no choice but to think she is ugly.

She came here believing—umm—oh crum—
I can't remember the seventh one—   ‡

> (Kur and Gal hold Helen in their arms, crooning to
> her, singing the Fairy chant, Isis, Inanna, Demeter,
> Kali, etc., giving her sips of water and nibbles
> of the plant, fanning her and petting her, and
> dressing her in a gorgeous gold and white, or
> perhaps salmon and deep blue, gown they have
> brought with them.[3] They help her off the bar,
> where she staggers center stage, wobbling. Exeunt
> Kur and Gal, gaily. Ereshkigal acts surprised
> to see her back on her feet.)

Helen

I fell through a hole   †
in the eye of death;
I drew Zero's breath.

I went to where the wind lives—
I put my ear there.
I went down below.
Where the wind lives is chaos;
what the wind does is blow.

The center of the wind is paradox,
completely orderly and patterned,
a mathematical, coherent person
with a mind, even a soul.

The eye is a sheet of crystal
on the other side of time;
the sky is a paradigm.
I could see myself reflected
in my inner and my outer mind.

Deep in the eye of death
the light is never standing,
it's dancing, it's unfolding,
light is holding dark,
shy is holding bold,
everything is blowing hot
with cold;

and that glancing of
the light that is not standing,
that speculating,
is the partnership we have
with death that is not, is
not dying, is glowing,
is chancing.

I'm no longer lying
in my cave of glass, I'm rocking,
I'm shaking,
I'm expanding

knowing flesh with all its names
is just a lovely little screen,
a speckled net,
for keeping some particular thought
intact

while we do
such juggling in the light
as we can do,

the clumsy stancing
that we call our standing
and our falling
through the blowholes carefully provided
in the eye of death.

I went all the way to Zero,
leaned in Zero's door;
and you know what lives in there?
Absolutely everything—everything at all.

Ereshkigal

Speak, Helen. Speak into my ear.
Speak until you lose your fear.

> *(As Helen revives her strength she begins to revile*
> *Ereshkigal. Nothing offers Helen a glass of liquid*
> *or a glass pipe, which she flings to the floor*
> *where it shatters.)*

Helen

I thought I needed you,
I've had enough of you,
you're trying to own me,
you wish you *were* me;
my beauty is real,
you can't take it,
You—who are you!
You stripped me—

> *(Helen walks around furiously, followed by Crows.)*

Crows

You stripped me;   †

Crows

Stripped!

Helen (screaming at Ereshkigal)

Like a chevrolet parked too long on a side street.

Crows

Stripped!

Helen

Like a chicken in a restaurant
specializing in chicken kebob.

Crows

Stripped!

Helen

Like a woman alone in a hotel
with a guilty-looking stranger.

Crows
  Stripped!

Helen
  Like a new recruit in the army.

Crows
  Stripped!

Helen
  Like a corpse thrown from a car at midnight.

Crows
  Stripped!

Helen
  Like a house before its next paint job.

Crows
  Stripped!

Helen
  Like a turkey on his way to the crap game run by foxes.

Crows
  Stripped!

Helen
  Like a fur seal in fur seal clubbing season.   ↓

Ereshkigal
  I just remembered her seventh venial virtue.
  She thought she needed another person
  to guide her through her life.
  Is anything more tawdry
  than the end of a love affair between two people
  who had entirely different expectations?
  All right, all right, you're going!
  I can see that!
  I can't wait to get you out of here!
  I'm going to give you everything of yours
  and more than you bargained for.

        Recall! Recall! Recall! Recall!   †
        Heaven and earth are yours, Helen,

you'll be Queen of the May.[4]
Clarity of vision,
clarity of hearing, too, you'll be hearing voices.
You'll have such a memory, as
remembers the future,
try to explain to your friends how you know so
much about them! Measurement and number
belong to you, Helen, now
you'll have to be a teacher.
Curiosity and scholarship will be yours
and metaphor—
you'll be a scientist—and more—a seer—
looked up to by everyone,
pitied by none; half the population will blame
their troubles on you. You'll sometimes hate it.
Decision is yours, Helen, and forcefulness comes
with it; no more excuses. You'll be known as
a speaker of truth, and all your suffering
will be amusing since you'll know—
how absolutely it's for Nothing.
But you asked for it, so you're going to get it.
Consciousness especially will be yours,
and its sister conscience.
Use them to polish the apple of self-esteem.
Worst of all your beauty will increase
as you get older, even in your own eyes, along
with your stature. You'll never be able to retire.
Never to complain. Never to want, always to
have, to be a provider. You'll get tired.
Don't expect me to pity you.
All I ask in return is that you choose
another innocent one to take your place.
Someone who needs to count down to Zero!
Demons of guilt will go with you
to make sure you keep this pledge.
Don't expect me to call you.

We've met before; you know we'll meet again,
if not in this life, then in some other one.   ↓

> *(Helen leaves, leading a procession of seven Crow
> Demons; they climb up to the upper world.
> Ereshkigal sits in the chair upstage, with the little
> table, contemplative, facing the audience as the
> lights go down on her. She blows the candle out.
> Nothing blows all the other candles out. Lights rise
> on the street outside the Crow Bar. There on the
> street the procession meets Nin, plainly dressed,
> anxiously waiting for Helen.)*

Crow Demons *(beginning to grab Nin)*
Let's go, let's go.
Here's a likely one, let's take her.

Helen *(shoving Crows away)*
You can't take her,   †
she loves me.

When I bowed down so low,
she bowed down too.

Even when she couldn't find me
she stood beside me.

Even when she couldn't understand me
she stood by me.

Even when she couldn't stand me
she stood for me.

You can't take her,
I love her as a friend.

Because of her I know more
about being human;

more than "stand up for myself,"
I know "stand up for another woman."   ↓

> *(Nin and Helen embrace and begin talking excitedly
> to each other about recent events. Enki comes in,*

with Kur and Gal. He is dressed in fire-fighting
garb, with a crown of leaves around his head, and
so are the Fairies. Enki is carrying a fire hose. The
Crow Demons grab Kur and Gal.)

Crows

Let's take these!

Crow

They seem perfectly good for Nothing!

Crow

Let's take these little easier-to-carry
fairy ones!

Helen (pushing the Crows away)

You can't take them,
they saved me.

Enki

You can't take them,
I need them.

(Explaining to Helen.)

I'm on my way to put out a forest fire.

Nin

How generous of you to take the time.

Enki

Oh, you know, I feel responsible.
The god of lightning set it,
to win a bet we had he couldn't do it
in the rainy season, that he'd fizzle
like wet matches. Now we have to
take our hatchets and go help
put an end to Emerline.

Helen

Emerline?

Enki

The forest fire's name is Emerline.

Don't you name everything? I do.
Helps me remember who is who.

Helen

I thought a forest fire is what.
Not who.

Enki

Who is what, ever think of that?   †
Ever think you might be *what*
(you think you're not)
instead of *who*
(you think you are)?

Consider all the names based on
occupations—Baker, Walker,
Carpenter, Fisher, Swisher—
if who you are is what you do,
and no one in your family does it any more?
Or if what you are is a star—
you could be Venus, of the evening,
traveling toward the dawn,
or you could just be called
"traveling toward the dawn"
and would you be a what, then,
or a who—I mean, is a what
changeable or is it personable?
When people say you're not who you used to be,
what if what they mean is true?
What became of the rest of who is you?

Ever wish upon a star?
Imagine if you couldn't call it by its name.
Imagine if you only knew how far away it is,
and its specific gravity; what would you wish for?

Is a plant a what?
Is a ghost a who?
Imagine thinking that a made-up television character
is a real person but your dog is not.

Is who a house cat but not a laboratory rat?
Is what a rock—then what is Mr. Spock?
Is a street who if it has a name
and what if it has a number?
Try to remember
what you've been
and who you've been seen in the person of;
is a person the sum of its parts?
Try to count yourself in instead of out.

Some people personify, others quantify.

Measuring the mettle of a person
or measuring the person of a metal
or meddling in the meter of a motor
or metaling the measure of a mother,
would you lose some of the stars you see
if you could count them only by their names?
Is counting a way of praying?

If what you really are is a number, say,
of conscious blobs of luminous light,
incandescing through your coat of flesh,
filling the entire viewing lens,
for a while, before your time to set,
then is consciousness a what?
An ability to see from far enough away
to count yourself out instead of in?

And isn't it true
that tax collectors created names
so they'd know what to do with who?
Then why is who's who any more than what's what?
Can you tell me that?   ↓

Helen
    You're driving me crazy
    with all your assumptions,
    you're driving me nuts with your qualifications.
    I'm leaving, I'm going to my own house,

my own possessions,
and my own point of view.

Crow Demons
Let's go, let's go,
let's go to Helen's own house!

*(All exeunt, Enki and Kur and Gal in a different
direction; Nin and Helen arm in arm.)*

SCENE THREE: ABOVEWORLD

Venus Shines Triumphant

Home of THOMAS *and* HELEN *Bull. It is near dawn.* THOMAS *is at
home with his new girlfriend* GISHI, *who, if possible, looks like him.
The place is a mess, things are oddly placed, and somehow gray or
white instead of their real color—sterile, frozen, wrapped in cloth.*
THOMAS *still has his telescope set up;* GISHI *sits in his lap while he
makes notes. Enter* HELEN, *with* NIN *and the seven* CROW DEMONS;
THOMAS *jumps up.*

Thomas
Helen, where have you been?
You're disgraceful—leaving me here to fend
for myself, and to tend your home fires.

Helen
You—who are you?   †
You're the one who didn't notice I was missing,
never saw me
going down, never thought I might have crashed,
never wondered, never asked,
never missed me, never mourned.
You're the one who assumed my absence

meant you were in charge of the whole bash;
yours is the head
swelling up underneath my crown.
Yours is the big dead end
sweating upon my throne.
You never tried to find me,
you found a silly replacement.
You're the one who's disgraceful.
I'll tell you what's what, now that we know you
for who you are, you're the one of my choice;
you're next,
you're going to break, and risk;
you're going down, you're going for a spin,
you're the very very very next one!   ⸸

Crows

Let's go, let's go! You're going with us!

Crow

Grab him, grab him by the horns.
Grab him, grab him, grab him by the tail.

Thomas

I haven't got a tail!

Crow (flirtatious)

Honey, everybody has a tail.

Thomas (avoiding the Demons)

You can't take me, I'm married to a goddess!   †
I'm married to a princess,
I'm married to Venus.
I live in a castle.
Can't you see what a successful man
I am?

You can't take me—
I'm a scientist,
I don't believe in demons—
I see you as illogical, irrational
figments of a savage

imagination—aaaeeee—
take your icy fingers off my arm!   ↓

Gishi (clinging to Thomas)
You can't take him!
He can't take it!
He's too tender—
I'll go with him,
I'll go for him,
I'll go mend him.
He can't take it! I'll go
with him—
you might break him.
I'm not fragile,
I'm not worth it—

Helen
Take her too—she's driving me crazy,
she's making me nervous,
she's making me violent!

> (*Crow Demons lead Thomas and Gishi off; they are
> clinging together. Helen, her anger abating, is
> visibly upset by Thomas going, although it is clear
> she will not change her mind.*)

Crow (to Thomas)
You're going to be King.

Thomas
King—really?

Crow
Crow-King!

Crows
CAW CAW CAW

Gishi
Where are we going?

Crows
Nowhere special, Nothing to worry about.

Nin

> Don't they look just like Hansel and Gretel? [1]
> Are you sending Thomas to a Lesbian bar?

Helen

> Our lady of the Underground   †
> is a very shape-shifting old crone,
> she's related to Mercury, or a wishing stone.
> You could call her a storm and not be wrong;
> you could call her a dirt god with a dirt god's
> habits, and be right on target.
> You could call her a song of living time,
> or death's wind chime.
> By the time anyone gets down there
> to be her student,
> she's likely to be a boxing trainer
> for the CIA, with a Theosophist bent,
> or a Zen Buddhist with a PhD
> in the physical sciences. Everyone's
> shadows are custom-made
> by their own needs.   ‡

> *(Nin gathers a stack of books and begins*
> *reading to Helen.)*

Nin

> Venus is the morning star now.
> She ought to be visible from where we are.
> She spent two months turning over.
> Now she'll be morning star for six months
> before disappearing again.

Helen

> Sounds like me. I was gone two months
> though it seemed
> I went for seven years . . . as though time
> is a series of events that mark us
> like tree rings.

Nin (reading)

> Venus rules Taurus the Bull.

Helen

I'm not so sure I want to rule bull.

Nin

Are you serious?

Helen

No, I'm only Venus. You can be Sirius.

Nin (reading)

Venus rules Libra, the balancing scale.

Helen (looking into the hand mirror)

To hang in the balance and remember what we've been;   †
to hang at the corner of the ceiling
and recall what we have dreamed;
not to be a maid—to be Joan of Arc—
the Maid, a warrior Maid,
to lead armies, nations,
pilgrimages, scientific expeditions
into the starry landscapes of the brain—
and the heart's brain.
To seek with all our intelligence and then
to find! to find!
to define, to map—
and to do more than understand,
to stand in the center of my own mind.
To combine
the inner, with the outer, whole . . .
now that's a science worth working for.   ‡

Nin

Beauty without truth is only wishful,
a fantasy, the false posturing of a fool.

Helen (looking through telescope)

The sky is a sheet of crystal
and time is what we are.
Venus shines triumphant in the morning sky.
Oh—I didn't know she looked like that, so near.
So beautiful, so forceful and so bright.

My eyes can hardly bear
to look at her.

Nin

Truth without beauty is ugly
and unbearably cruel.

Helen

The telescope's mirrors catch the light
and bring the image, not the object, near.
Everything we see we see in symbols—
what Thomas ever was to me
and I to him . . . was our metaphor for marriage.

Nin

Venus is luminous
but veiled. We never completely
see her. We never see her bare.

Helen (training the telescope on the audience; at times she stops looking through it to address Nin directly)

She's veiled, but I believe I know   †
what's under there.
The dark side of the mirror
is what is real.
To be completely in the dark
is to seek reality—the as-yet-unformed.
All else is metaphor—or worse,
is Thomas fantasizing Venus,
loving to measure himself against her parameters—
the image is a reflection of the shadow of the real.
We all use mirrors to trap the light,
the drawing of the light into an image,
the sorting of the images into a symbol,
the weaving of the symbols into a metaphor,
the gathering of the metaphors into a group of metaphors—
a metaform, a myth,
a play of light on surfaces,
to which we bring our suffering, joy, anger—
terror.

*(Helen shrieks playfully as she plays the telescope
around on the audience.)*

Oh what's out there, what's out there?

*(There is a knock on the door. Nin goes to answer
while Helen continues with telescope.)*

I too know how to use mirrors,
how to weave with lights and sound.
How to see from at least two points of view,
a parallax of measurement.
And I know how to recognize my own being
in the dark side of the wind . . .   ↓

*(Nin comes back with a gift box. Helen
unwraps it.)*

Nin
Something for you.
From Thomas?

Helen
No, he always sends flowers. Daisies.
This is from Ereshkigal, with a note of thanks.
He arrived in her domain. And safely.
I'm so glad.

(Wiping tears from her eyes.)

I was more worried about him
than I was letting on.

Nin (seeing the present—a large black stone horse)
Now that's substantial.

(There is the distant sound of brass wind chimes.)

Helen
An onyx horse.
I wonder if I know what to do with it.

Nin
Of course you do.

Helen
Of course I do.

"It isn't as simple as it may seem
to poison the apple of self-esteem."

(She gives the horse a central position among the
smaller glass horses, on a table, center stage, pauses
thoughtfully, then addresses it.)

Helen

O Lady, Lady of the changing shapes,   †
help me remember
how to dance in place;
when to witness,
when to harness,
when to charge with all my forces.

I don't know the reaches of my fate.
I know your shadow falls across my face.

O Lady, Lady of the Great Below.
Hard are your lessons,
many-fanged your harshness;
irresistible are your passions
and sweet, sweet are your praises.

I don't know the mazes of your soul.
I know your shadow falls beside me
everywhere I go.   ‡

(The dawn continues brightening as Nin reads from
factual "hard science" books on mathematics and
new physics while Helen dusts, unwraps, and
straightens, her motions drawing attention to the
presence of large treelike plants, an enormous
globe, models of cities and other things that suggest
that her house is the universe itself, rather than a
simple house. Slow curtain.)

T W O
P O E M S

Descent to the Roses of the Family

Open Letter to My Brother on the Subject of Family Pride

1
Last Thanksgiving when our old father,
wrapped in the lap robe I gave him one Christmas,
gathered his family around his knees
to tell us what heritage we had from him—
he said, "The reason the white people are superior,
is that the white people are the only human beings"—
and I fell.

I saw each of us falling
into the gall of old habits
my own frightened silence
my father's descent to drunkenness
the whip he makes of his tongue
the lash marks in our skin of memories
the peg of neglect and need we're hanging on
no one ever comes to take us down

Our father of the tender moustache
Our father of the immigrant's bitterness
Our father of the woodcarving hands
Our father of weeping when the kitten died
Our father of whistling beloved songs

129

Our father of providing steak and doughnuts
Our father of the well-told story
Our father of the embracing T-shirt
Our father of the murderous impulse

Our eyes never leave his face,
our smiles hooking for his approval
(that never arrives).
When we see a child helpless before us
we are likely to blossom into rage,
sticks planted into the dirt of experience.
We turn fury, judge and jury,
our arms fall and rise.
Whips shape our tongues.
All we have known
we pass on.

> This is the legacy of the white race
> that I will remember long after my death:
> that it beats its children
> that it blunts itself with alcohol
> that its women suffer from a blight: passivity
> that it carries a gun

2
At the family gathering
I notice how the children sit—all of us—
remarkably still,
two generations watch
as battered children will
for any twitch or clue.
Our sister's son the worst,
unable to speak without her
cutting him in two
(after she left home she hated men
for years she told me).
She raised him alone.

He watches her face
the way your son watches you.

Our mother watches the mind inside
her own mind.
She perpetually falls out of time.
She goes to Venus.
At six I became a desperate clown
to keep her here.
I have learned to talk to her
for several sentences in a line
by tugging on her starry wall,
howling down her tunnel.
I still need so to be planted
in her garden dirt. O my brother,
tell me what lives over on the planet Venus
more pressing than our childhood Earth?

As I sometimes do, you treat her
like a lovable imbecile.
Unable to escape the mirror of her face
our sister is outfront cruel.

3
Well at least you're a white man
yes at least you've got that
and it gives you something, a word to say
for what you're not—
and that's saying a lot

I was forbidden to say the word
by my mother, who has forbidden herself
to say it, children couldn't say it,
though my father
often said it, twenty times a day at times,
certainly more than he said other words,
"I love you," for instance, or

"You did that just right,"
and being a drunk my father is free
to say any words he wants.

Between the two of them,
the father and the mother,
we had a lot of talk about nigger
in our family, and then we had
a lot of talk about forbidden.
Because I am trying now to really listen
I notice some of the meanings, hidden:

    nigger is a black core of action
    you don't dare take for yourself
    nigger is the intense motion
    chained up in your chest
    nigger is the bold center
    of the forbidden rose
    forbidden begins
    with the lips pressed tight together
    and the eyes half-closed
    forbidden to move the hips
    shoulders and thighs
    forbidden to laugh out loud
    forbidden to draw pictures in the air
    with the face and hands
    forbidden to shout, to talk a great deal
    forbidden to whistle
    to sing in the street, to exult, to go hallelujah
    to bend over in half, laughing
    to slap the knee
    forbidden to tongue language
    in a living form
    forbidden to hunker down
    to roll the eyes in terror
    or mock derision
    forbidden to know how to curse

someone all the way down the block
nigger is the moving center
in the bright red rose.
Underneath forbidden
is the niggerrose.

4
You tell stories, my brother,
about black people in your town, how
"The niggers are likely to break in on you whenever they
feel like it," you say. Yet I know factually
for you they never have.
Who was always breaking in on you
was our white father.
"He threw your brother at the wall a few times,"
my sister told me.
"If you didn't say the right thing at dinner,
pow—across the mouth," you demonstrated for me once,
the sweeping backhand of parental terrorism.
I see your sweet
red bud of mouth in the childhood photos.
Now you tell me you're "afraid of niggers."
I don't believe you.
Oh, I know you have your feelings
and your scorn,
but I believe it's someone very white
and very close to you, who motivates
the thorn of your tongue.
I remember you telling me as we drove around town
how well you know the inside of the jail,
you've been in it three or four times.
"How could that be," I asked, "you've only
come to visit them
three or four times over the years."
"And every time," you said, "Dad insists
I drink with him and then I drink too much
and while I'm driving him home

I'm busted for drunk driving."
Well, at least you're alive but
free?
You were fifty-three years old my brother
when you told me this—and your father eighty-five.

You were the one pegged for scapegoat in the family.
Though I was the lesbian, the "black sheep," you call it.
Read: a little reminiscent of a nigger.
You were the one brave and strong enough
to play bad boy and drunk, the one with dirt
on his hands
so the women could be clean and
patient self-enduring righteous white flowers,
not saying the wrong words,
just too stupid to understand the machinations
of a man's world.
You were the one beaten the most, chastised, stigmatized,
turned over to the cops to teach you
a lesson. No wonder your mouth leaks every kind of hatred,
trying to break through the gate of deaf ears.

Our mother is a white rose
bled down to a ghost.
When I say she is a ghost
I mean she lives on Venus,
mostly, fled there long ago—
Our mother has deaf ears
to what she doesn't want to hear
and this is almost everything.
When I enter my mother I find her center
is a black core
of madness
black as the iris of her eye.
Black as the dried blood at the corner of a
child's mouth, your rosebud mouth
my brother. Black as the blood
soaked into my childhood pillow

of hour on bloody hour my body
howling for attention
through my nose.
Our mother is a white rose
bled down to a ghost.

5
The women in our family are considered
stupid. After two days of listening to the men deliver
nigger jokes and gun stories,
Indian jokes, queer stories and whore stories I too
am stupid. I don't mention that I'm teaching
college, now. You say that you inherited
Dad's "quickness," and you say
I didn't—I'm more like Mom.
Since Mom, especially in gatherings,
withdraws to silent deafness
(they don't talk to human beings on Venus)
I don't take this as a compliment.
Unable to escape the mirror
I sneer.
I live in fear.

My mother's descent to madness
to stupefaction
the blue haze inside the iris of her eyes
the paleness of her face, the gauze of death
over her emotions, the paralysis.
Her refusal to protect me
her absence, the absence of her expression,
the absence in her person
my terror of the bottomless depths
of the depression in her eyes
my mother's denial of her own wildness, our denial
of her atrocity, of her neglect
of her vindictive punishment
our collective belief in her innocence.

135

The thorn of her absolute will
that runs me through
whenever I enter her center,
unguarded. How she sent him—
a bull to do her roaring.
She sent my father to do the torment
in her stead.
She sent him, she sent my father
to do the torment in her stead.
She, my mother, sent him
(in her descent to absence)
to do the torment
in her stead.

And he put his hands upon me but I did not fear
he put his angry thoughts upon me but I did not fear
and of course I feared
but I did not feel the fear.
I did not feel anything at all.

    This is the legacy of the white rose
    that I will remember long after my death:
    that its beaten children beat their children
    that it calls alcohol "spirits"
    that its women offer their passivity to their families
    like a whip.

    6
    nigger is a strong feeling
    on its own in the world
    nigger is a black core of anger
    you don't directly dare expose
    nigger is the forbidden passion
    running out of your nose
    nigger is the electric middle
    of the emotional rose
    forbidden begins with the heart closed
    and the throat clamped shut

forbidden begins with the belly flat and still.
forbidden to spit and to feel
your angry opinion spin free
forbidden to roll, to be large-hearted
and to stand short and bending
as well as straight and tall
forbidden to do more than stand stiff,
to *under*stand,
to fall
to turn face up to the laughing sky
and nearly die
forbidden to cry
to sob on the street, to snuffle
to lie moaning on the dear cruel earth
forbidden to stroke flesh, even our own
forbidden to ken life's ordinary wildness
repression begins with the hips locked up
and the mind closed
nigger is a treasure store of your own emotions
forbidden expression
the black wet velvet center
of the paralyzed
rose, stolen from you
from the start.
Under the thumb of forbidden
beats the niggerheart.

I remember our father gambling,
how he failed at gambling;
his broad gestures, his big red nose.
I remember him saying *Be* there! *Be* there!
Be there! as he slapped the cards down.
I remember him being a clown.

Our father of welcoming grins.
Our father of fantastic hopefulness.
Our father of slumped in the doorway.

I remember his face ashen when he
didn't bring a thing home,
not even a silly teddy bear,
when he lost himself in the crap game
of his own decisions.
I remember our father laughing,
his hands drawing pictures in the air,
and crying; and you tell me he kicked
a plate glass window in and was hauled off
more than once to jail.

Well at least
he's a drunkard
yes at least he's got that, at least
our father has passion—
some facsimile. He gets his mind back
when he's sober. At least he's there.
I don't remember our mother crying
or gambling, or singing, or raging.
I remember her lips pressed together
and her hands in a tight vise-hold
on the arms of her madly rocking
rocking chair.
Our mother is controlling
and controlled.

7
My own descent to depression
the blue haze in my mother's eyes
the bottomless gauze of depression
my descent into the wound of it

My own descent into the blue gauze
of my mother's gaze
the absence of her presence
her absence I filled by
falling into it
my descent into the dull pits

of her pupils
my falling endlessly through the dark
the internal cloud of my mother's own madness

No one has ever robbed me
and many, yes many have robbed me,
but no one has ever robbed me
as this has robbed me
my own recurrent paralysis
the grip of the blue haze
its clutch at my heart
the dying feeling, the not caring
the days on end of it
the weeks, the years left out of themselves
the blue gauze shield that has grown
over my heart
my absence to myself, my deafness,
my absence to love
lifted only by some meanness, some anger
my father's meanness
the whip of his voice
the whip of his voice in my voice
cutting through the dread stillness
of my own descent to Venus
cutting the nothing, shredding,
rousing me at last
to some amount of bleeding, to some feeling,
enough to continue

For protection my brother
you tell me to get a gun—
we are a family with many guns—
and it is true I am angry.
Yet who would you have me shoot, our old father?
My mother that she refused to protect
or did not properly care for us?
Should I shoot her madness? His whiskey bottles
endlessly hidden and battled over?

Whose death can give me freedom from
my own frightened silence?
Who can I shoot that can return my childhood to me?
I am afraid of violence against my person.
I am more afraid of going mad, of withdrawing.
I'm most afraid of living with torment all my life.
I'm completely afraid of my own passivity.
Who, besides myself, can I shoot to solve any of this?

8
What happens when the women abdicate their powers,
and let the red rose go
in favor only of the white.
What happens when women let the red rose
of passion go, when they go soldier in a thin-
lipped line of disapproval, silence,
hips as still as if the iron belt of chastity
wrapped them still.
As though the burning times took everyone
in Europe with some blood in her, left the rest of us
with ash, ash of what we were.
What happens when women
try to rule by being ruled by others
and by being "good."
Our mother is not good. And not an angel.
In fact the times her thorny stick is planted
in the solid dirt she's an entire woman.
Our father is not
bad. And no devil.
In fact without the surge to hit and scrape
he's rather human.
Take away the battery, the arrogance and the alcohol
and down would come innocence
woodpile and all.

   This is the legacy of the white rose
   that I will remember long after my death:
   that it hides the dirt under its fingernails

    that it calls fingernail dirt "nigger"
    that it thinks it can grow roses without fingernail dirt.

Which brings me to the women.
See us three females in the photo—
aren't we quiet? Aren't we nice?
Nothing nigger in the picture,
unless you count my dike clothes,
or the bizarre black and silver light
behind our mother's eyes
(shadow of the planet Venus).
Or my sister's fury,
her refusal to be generous
in the face of neglect.
My mother is a white rose
bled down to a ghost,
and behind the gauze of ghost,
a vision, behind the deafness,
words spoken from another planet, age, rhythm,
behind the madness, splendor of the cosmos,
real spirits
and a multitude of lives like multicolored leaves,
unfolding.

9

Our mother was warned, my sister said, not to marry him,
"everybody said it." He was a gambler—a drunkard,
a no-good—everybody knew it.
Our parents' early pictures show a raucous bold
couple, certain of themselves and their superiority
over others. My mother believed she could control
his monster—arrogance beyond belief.
My mother believed she shouldn't express anger,
and he graciously
agreed to do it for her.

Our father of no belief.

Oh brother, I don't want you to be the one
to do my violence
oh my brother I can do my own
if there is violence to be done I can be the one to do it
and to choose not to do it.

nigger is a black core of creation
you don't directly dare explore
the spirit voice inside your middle ear
the quasar hole
in the American soul
nigger is the forbidden impression
boiling at mid-Earth
nigger is the black hole of unprediction
in the carnivorous rose, a glorious garden
of the unknown and unknowable
the who-knows-what's-going-to-happen-next
nigger is the unexplained and inexplicable
the unpredictable, the suddenness
of surrender to anything is possible, the seven
come eleven or the snake eyes in the roll
nigger is a handful of cards in the alley
the sweet piercing lyric inside the trombone's growl
the stark desire you have in your heart on a Saturday
afternoon and follow it all over town, until
you meet a beautiful Venus and fall in love with her
one time, and another time she takes you
for a terrible fall
nigger is a clown spirit walking beside you
or plagues that sweep across continents pruning,
pruning, pruning us one and all
a vision magnetizing your whole life's goal
in the form of a black hole opening before you
nigger is my own terror
nigger is everything we do not have
whenever we think we have it all
under control.

DESCENT TO THE ROSES OF THE FAMILY

Under the forbidding/forbidden soul of America
lives the niggersoul.

My own descent to find my violence
a white woman searching her depths
looking for her corruptions, seeking them

Wanted: all my own violences to
come home to me
all my own committed atrocities
to come heap themselves in a shitpile
on my doorstep
a pile of roses of every description.
I might hate some of them
but at least they'll be here with me,
yes at least I'll have that.

I don't want my atrocities pacing the streets
without me
shrouded in rags, sores, and madness
over the bodies of dark and white-skinned men and women
staggering the streets of Berkeley
and the Upper West Side of Manhattan,
and the wide boulevards of the capital city,
kicking in windows
to balance with evil the scale for the sinless:
the nice polite determinedly "cancer-free"
hands on the nice
polite wheat sandwiches
with not too many calories
and not too much insecticide
and not too much MSG
and a neutral-colored rose—just one—
in a glass
on the table

Oh my brother
our family's descent
to find its roses
the despair of our denial, our roselessness
the secret of dirt and what grows of it
the peg of need we're hanging on . . .

Talkers in a Dream Doorway

You leaned your body in the doorway
(it was a dim NY hall)
I was leaving as usual—on my way.
You had your head cocked to the side
in your most intelligent manner
eyes glistening   with provocation,
gaze direct as always,
and more, as though wanting something,
as though I could have bent and kissed you
like a lover
and nothing social would have changed,
no one minded, no one bothered.
I can't testify to your intention.

I can only admit to my temptation.

Your intensity dazed me, so matter of fact
as though I could have leaned my denser body into yours,
in that moment while the cab waited
traffic roaring nine flights down
as well as in my ears,
both of us with lovers of our own
and living on each end of a large continent.
We were raised in vastly different places,
yet speak this uncanny similar tongue.
Some times we're different races,
certainly we're different classes,
yet our common bonds and common graces,

common wounds and destinations
keep us closer than some married folks.

I admit I have wanted to touch your face, intimately.

Supposing that I were to do this awful
act, this breach of all our lovers' promises—in reality—
this tiny, cosmic infidelity: I believe our lips would first be
tentative, then hardened in a rush of feeling, unity
such as we thought could render up the constellations AND our
daily lives, justice, equality AND freedom,
give us worldly definition
AND the bread of belonging. In the eye of my imagination
I see my fingers curled round the back of your head
as though it were your breast
and I were pulling it to me.
As though your head were your breast
and I were pulling it to me.

I admit, I have wanted to possess your mind.

I leaned forward to say good-bye,
aware of your knuckle possibly digging a tunnel
through my thigh, of the whole shape of your body as
an opening, a doorway to the heart.
Both of us with other lives to lead
still sure why we need so much to join,
and do join with our eyes on every
socially possible occasion.
More than friends, even girl friends,
more than comrades, surely,
more than workers with the same bent,
and more than fellow magicians
exchanging recipes for a modern brand of golden spit.

I admit we have already joined more than physically.

The cab's horn roars.
You smile, or part your lips as if to welcome how I'd just
slip in there, our tongues nodding together,
talking inside each other's mouth for a change,
as our upper bodies talked that night we danced together.
Your face was wine-flushed, and foolish; my desire selfish,
pushing you beyond your strength.
You paid for it later, in pain, you said.
I forget you are older, and fragile. I forget your arthritis.
I paid later in guilt, though not very much.
I loved holding you so close, your ear pressed to my ear.
I wanted to kiss you then but I didn't dare
lest I spoil the real bonding we were doing there.

I admit I have wanted to possess my own life.

Our desire is that we want to talk of really important things,
and words come so slowly, eons of movement
squirt them against our gums. Maybe once in ten years a
    sentence
actually flashes out, altering everything in its path.
Flexing our tongues into each other's dreams, we want to
suck a new language, strike a thought into being, out of the old
fleshpot. That rotten old body of our long submersion. We sense
the new idea can be a dance of all kinds of women,
one we seek with despair and desire
and exhaltation; are willing to pay for
with all-consuming passion, AND those tiny boring paper cuts.
I never did lean down to you that day.
I said good-bye with longing and some confusion.

I admit to wanting a sword AND a vision.

I doubt I will ever kiss you in that manner.
I doubt I will ever stop following you around, wanting to.
This is our love, this stuff
pouring out of us, and if this mutual desire is

some peculiar ether-marriage
among queens, made of the longing of women
to really love each other, made of dreams
and needs larger than all of us,
we may not know what to do
with it yet but at least
we've got it,
we're in the doorway.
We've got it right here, between us,

(admit it) on the tip of our tongues.

Appendix 1: The Descent of Inanna to the Underworld

Translation of the Sumerian Text by
Sara Denning-Bolle and Daniel A. Foxvog;
Poetic Rendering by Betty De Shong Meador

1

SHE	in great heaven turned her ear to great earth
THE GODDESS	in great heaven turned her ear to great earth
INANNA	in great heaven turned her ear to great earth
MY LADY	left heaven abandoned earth went down below
INANNA	left heaven abandoned earth went down below

where she ruled the city
she left
where she ruled the temple
she left

SHE WENT DOWN BELOW

Seven cities and their temples are named, with the chorus "she went down below." These include descriptions, "An's temple Eanna," "land's halo temple," "sky terrace temple," "measured garden temple," "throne-dias temple," "mountain land temple," and "little flower temple." She left each of these and she went down below.

seven sacred powers bound to her side
sacred powers gathered in her hand
sacred powers firm under foot
she left

she wound a crown of pure cloth
crown of the wild steppe
on her head
a beauty shone through hair locks on her brow

she held the lapis measuring reed
and coiled the royal field rope in her hands

at her neck she tied lapis beads
twin egg-stones filled her breast

gold ring on her hand
breastplate *man-come-come*
she wrapped herself in regal robes
the perfume *may-he-come* trailed after her glance

INANNA WENT DOWN BELOW

2

Inanna's chosen minister, Ninshubur, follows her. Inanna calls her "my rock," "carrier of true words," and instructs her to stay in the world above:

I am going down below
when I reach that place
    wail for me
    cry in lamentation by the ruins
    play a drum song
    drum for me in the throne court
    wander for me
    wander through the houses of the gods

    tear at your eyes
    tear at your mouth
    tear at that unspeakable place

    wear rags for me
    only rags

Then Inanna instructs Ninshubur further: go alone to the houses of each of three gods, beginning with Enlil.

enter Enlil's great mountain house
look him in the eye and
WEEP

say
    father Enlil
    do not let anyone
    hold your daughter down below

    do not let your
    good silver
    mix with the dust of that place

do not let your
precious lapis lazuli be
split with the mason's stone

do not let your sweet
boxwood be
sawn with the carpenter's wood

do not let the maiden
Inanna
be held down below

if Enlil does not help you
go to Ur

At Ur Ninshubur is to repeat the same entreaty to Nanna the moon god in his temple "house-of-light." When Nanna does not help you, Inanna says, go to the temple of the wisdom god Enki and make your supplication to him. Inanna says:

wise father Enki
lord of wide ear
who knows the life-giving plant
who knows the life-giving water
he is the one
to restore me
to life

I go
Ninshubur
do not follow

go
Ninshubur
do what I say
do not forsake
the word I speak

Appendix One

3

At the netherworld gate of Ganzir Inanna cries. "Open UP, *Doorman, open up the house, Neti, I am alone,* LET ME IN.*" Neti, great doorman of the netherworld, answers:*

    YOU
    who are you?

I am Inanna
star of evening
traveling toward the dawn

YOU
Inanna
star of evening
traveling toward the dawn
    why are you here
    in the land-of-no-return
    what led your heart
    where no traveler turns back?

"I have come for pure Ereshkigal, my older sister," Inanna replies. She tells Neti that she has come down for the funeral of her sister's husband Gugalanna, the Great Bull of Heaven. Neti tells her to wait while he speaks to his queen, Ereshkigal. Once in the house of Ereshkigal, Neti, addressing her as "my queen," describes the visitor at the gate, including the seven powers bound to her side, sacred powers gathered at her hand, sacred powers firm under her foot. He describes her seven badges of office: the cloth over her brow, lapis lazuli necklace, coiled measuring line and rod, twin egg-stones at her breast, gold ring, breastplate (named "man-come-come"), royal robes, and the perfumed mascara "may-he-come."

INANNA IS HERE BELOW

Ereshkigal
slaps her thighs
bites at her lips

says

    Neti
    great doorman of the netherworld
    come here
    listen
    do exactly what I say

    bolt the seven gates of the netherworld
    then
    one by one
    open each door
    open each door
    of the Palace Ganzir

    let her come in
    capture her
    strip off her clothes
    carry them away
    bring her to me

Neti follows her instructions exactly, and at each gate, as Inanna passes through, someone removes one of the badges of her queenly office: cloth, lapis beads, twin egg-stones, breastplate, gold ring, coiled measuring line, and queenly robe. At each stripping she asks, "What is this?" and Neti replies: "Be silent Inanna, sacred customs must be fulfilled. Do not open your mouth against this rite."

When Inanna is "naked and bowed low," someone brings her to Ereshkigal, who rises from her wooden throne, and Inanna sits on the throne in her place. Seven judges of the underworld, the An-nunaki, fix on her the death eye, shout at her the wrath words, cry out "Sacrilege!"

they beat the doomed woman
into a piece of meat
hang her rotting flesh
on a peg

4
three days and three nights pass

During this time Ninshubur, Inanna's chosen minister, wails for her as she was instructed, crying in lamentation, playing the shem *drum in the throne court, wanders for her through the houses of the gods, tearing at her eyes, mouth, and "unspeakable place," wearing only rags of grief for the goddess of the sky. According to instruction she proceeds to Enlil's great mountain temple, where, weeping, she entreats him:*

father Enlil
do not let anyone
hold your daughter down below

do not let your
good silver
mix with the dust of that place

do not let your
precious lapis lazuli be
split with the mason's stone

do not let your sweet
boxwood be
sawn with the carpenter's wood

do not let the maiden
Inanna
be held down below

Enlil is enraged, responding that Inanna wants great heaven and also wants great earth below. He says that desires for netherworld powers are forbidden, that whoever seizes them is doomed to stay below, and asks, "Who would ever want to come back from that place anyway?" Since he will not help, Ninshubur goes next to the temple of the moon god Nanna, repeating her entreaty, and he responds ex-

actly as Enlil did. When she goes to the third temple, that of the wisdom god Enki, and goes through her plea for help, he responds sympathetically, "My daughter, what has she done, I am deeply troubled," repeating four variations of this.

he takes dirt
from under his fingernail
makes a *kurgarra*

he takes dirt
from a second fingernail
makes a *galaturra*

Enki gives the kurgarra *the life-giving plant and the* galaturra *the life-giving water, and instructs them to go below:*

at the great wooden door
fly around like flies
sneak through the door cracks like demons

there Ereshkigal
great with child
lies moaning

no linen covers
her pure body

nothing binds
her full-vessel breasts

she rakes at her body
with ax-sharp claws

her hair tangles on her head
like leeks

when she cries
my womb-heart
oh my womb-heart

say to her
    our Lady
    you are troubled
    oh your poor womb-heart

when she moans
my liver-soul
oh my liver-soul

say to her
    our Lady
    you are troubled
    oh your poor liver-soul

then she will say
    WHO ARE YOU
    who cries with the pain in my womb-heart
    who moans with the pain in my liver-soul

    if you are gods
    let me promise you something

    if you are men
    let me change your fate

make her swear to this
by the breath of heaven
by the life of earth

stay then
now you are safe

even if she offers you
a river to drink
do not accept it

even if she offers you
a field of grain to eat
do not accept it

say to her
        give us the beaten flesh
        hanging on that peg

she will answer
        that beaten flesh
        is your queen

say
        whether our king
        or our queen
        give it to us

she will give you
the beaten flesh
hanging on the peg

spread
over the flesh
the life-giving plant

pour
over the flesh
the life-giving water

Inanna
will
rise up

The galaturra *and the* kurgarra *obey Enki's instructions, flying around the great wooden door like flies, sneaking through the door cracks like demons, and finding the naked Ereshkigal in birth pains just as Enki had said, they deliver their sympathetic words, and she grants them any favor. When they ask for the beaten flesh she gives it to them, and they pour the life-giving plant and the life-giving water over her.*

INANNA
RISES UP

holy Ereshkigal
says
to the *galaturra*
to the *kurgarra*

> carry
> your queen
> away

5
Inanna
leaves the netherworld

the plan of Enki
freed her

on her way
as she is leaving
the Annunaki seize her

stop
they say
no one can leave
the netherworld
unscathed

Inanna
for you to leave
give us
a head
for your head

holy Inanna
ascends

And the underworld judges, the Annunaki, go with her, along with small and large demons like fence reeds and like fenceposts; they go looking for her substitute, to go down in her place. They come first to the faithful minister Ninshubur, who wears rags and rolls in the dust. The demons shout, "Go, Inanna, to your city, we will take this one away." But Inanna lists the faithful deeds of Ninshubur, how she wailed and drummed and tore at her body in grief and went alone to each of the houses of the gods seeking help. "She is the one who gave me my life," Inanna says, "I will never give her to you." The judges then take her to Shara, who also wears rags and rolls in the dust in mourning for Inanna, and the judges again say, "Inanna, go to your city, we will take this one"; but Inanna answers, "Shara is my singer, who sings my praises and cuts my nails and combs my hair, I will never give him to you." Next the judges go to Lulal, her "honey-man," who drops at her feet, wears rags and rolls in the dust. Again the judges try to take him and again Inanna defends him, "Lulal is he who follows at my right and who follows at my left," she says, "I will never give him to you." Finally the judges take her to the steppe of the great apple tree:

there Dumuzi
her husband
sits on a splendid throne
wears a magnificent robe

the demons
grab at his thighs

seven
pour milk from his churn
demons lunge at him
smite his head

he is stricken
the shepherd
lays down
his long reed flute
Dumuzi
lays down
his single-reed pipe

Inanna
stares
the death eye

speaks
the wrath words

cries out
>SACRILEGE!

says
>CARRY
>HIM
>AWAY

>gives
>Dumuzi
>into their hands

Dumuzi turns pale, wails with terror, and prays to the sun god Utu, saying, "I am spouse of a goddess, I am not mortal, I prance on the holy knee of Inanna." He asks Utu to help him escape his demons by turning him into a snake, and in this disguise Dumuzi escapes the

demons. He flees to the house of his sister Geshtinanna, who hides
him, refuses to give him up even under torture, and then volunteers
to go down below in his place.

Dumuzi
is weeping

the queen
Inanna
finds him

Inanna
takes his hand

says

> half the year will be yours
> Dumuzi
> half the year your sister's
>
> on the day you set
> your sister will be seized
>
> on the day your sister sets
> that day
> you will be seized

Inanna
gives Dumuzi
in her place

HOLY ERESHKIGAL
SWEET IS YOUR PRAISE

Appendix 2: Background Notes on Characters in "The Queen of Swords"

INANNA: Sumerian Queen of Heaven and Earth. She is also Venus, which she indicates by saying "I am Inanna, traveling toward the dawn." This can be interpreted astronomically as the "descent of Venus" in the planet's periodic change from evening to morning star. Inanna is also associated with the sun, the greatest power of the daytime sky, and with the moon, the greatest power of the nighttime sky. Enheduanna, the earliest known individual poet, exalted Inanna at length in about 2300 B.C., and was a priestess of the moon temple.

Inanna's cycle of stories, of which the descent myth is only one, constitutes a great psychological drama with profound meanings for modern people, as well as being an invaluable sacred text revolving centrally around female characters whose attributes have figured prominently in the literatures of many cultures. Goddesses related to her in other contexts include Demeter, who turns the earth completely barren as she seeks help in getting her daughter Persephone out of the underworld; Freya, a Nordic goddess for whom Friday, Venus's day, was named; and the Egyptian goddess Isis, whose Dumuzi is named Osiris. Other goddesses with similar attributes are Ama-terasu, sun goddess of Japan; Iyeticu, corn goddess of certain American Pueblo Indians; and Oshun, a West African goddess of beauty and love.

ERESHKIGAL: Lady of the Great Below. As queen of the spirits of the dead in her palace of Ganzir (the desert), she is naked, shamanic, and ruthless, a counterpart of Kali, the Celtic Morrigan, Ceridwen, Hel, and other destroyers of the merely physical. She does not have an elegant metal and jeweled throne but a plain wooden one. With her *shem* drum, long fingernails, and tangled hair she is one with the truly ancient shaman figures such as Baubo, who bawdily confronted Demeter, or Uzume, who enticed the Japanese sun goddess Ama-terasu from her dark cave. In later stories Ereshkigal was villified, and her human counterparts were burned at the stake, tortured, and driven underground; she remained in variants of the Inanna stories as "the wicked queen," the "dark Morgan, Queen of Fairy" (Morgana Le Fay), "the evil stepmother," and so on. The black and red of anarchy and birth/death are her colors, as is purple, the color of transformation.

ENKI: His name means literally "God of the Earth." He is variously god of wisdom and sweet waters. I decided a jovial, generous-hearted nature god with a touch of eccentric physicist fit him best in "The Queen of Swords." He appears in more than one of the related Inanna myths. In his male aspect his "sweet waters" have been interpreted as fertilizing semen that permits the growth of plants in the arid Sumerian landscape around the Tigris and Euphrates rivers. Enki's city Eridu is located where these two rivers meet the Persian Gulf. He is a magician and master of ritual and incantation; he has a marvelous nurturing and drunkenly generous side. In his female aspect he is described as "pregnant" and perhaps at some earlier time he was completely female.

In the story called "Inanna and the God of Wisdom," a drunk and effusively generous Enki gives the young Inanna the gift of *me* (pronounced *may*). *Me* are groups of special god-powers. She decides to keep them, loading them into her great "boat of heaven" (an extended metaphor for her vulva). A sobered and more possessive Enki schemes to have them returned, but all his attempts are foiled by Inanna and her *sukkal* (powerful servant) Ninshubur. Inanna gives up her *me* to make her descent, and as a result of her gamble acquires additional powers of the underworld.

NINSHUBUR: Queen of the East. Wolkstein and Kramer, in *Inanna, Queen of Heaven and Earth,* read Ninshubur's role as servant to Inanna as representing "the inner spiritual resources of Inanna, which are intended for the greater good of Sumer" (p. 149). This is one interpretation I have tried to follow in "The Queen of Swords," of Nin (Ninshubur) as Helen's "higher mind," the ultimate good sense that will stop her short of total destruction or enslavement and make possible her ascent. In addition, Nin's role as friend seems to me particularly important for women at this time/space in our story.

NETI: The gatekeeper of Ereshkigal's domain of Ganzir greets Inanna, then is instructed by the Lady of the Great Below to let her pass through one gate at a time, stripping her, silencing her, and bending her low at each one. The word *neti* means "nothing" in Sanskrit. In numerology zero is the source of everything. This is particularly intriguing to me since Neti is the "higher mind" of Ereshkigal. (Or is it "lower mind"?) I conceive of Nothing in "The Queen of Swords" as genderless, a dealer in whatever brings us face to face with our own essential nothingness. More broadly, Nothing is the creative power of zero, the limitless possibility that yawns wide each time our circumstances or our inner attitudes change.

KURGARRA and GALATURRA: These two creations of the dirt under Enki's nails embody the profound principle of reducing everything to the truth of dirt, to the understanding of oneself as "nailed fast to the fat earth" (to quote a line from "Descent to the Butch of the Realm"), of needing always to return to Mater Materia for the basic knowledge from which wisdom grows. That they disguise themselves as flies or demons is particularly appropriate to their role of calling attention to elements despised (at our peril) that are actually sacred, vital, and sustaining of life.

The "trick" they use on Ereshkigal is empathy, commiseration. Many a con game has succeeded using the same trick. On the other hand empathy is a primary tool in healing of all kinds, especially in psychological therapy as well as in groups that commiserate about common oppressions, traumas, and addictions. In the throes of a gripping depression sometimes a single understanding sentence will trigger release, allowing our ascent to ordinary life on earth, with the usual accompanying heightened zeal of newly coming into a fresh understanding from a "below" place.

DUMUZI: The bull god consort and lover of Inanna is a character of great fascination to me; he has an extensive history which is not even hinted at in my play, where he takes a minor part. The last quarter at least of the text of "The Descent of Inanna to the Underworld" tells of Dumuzi's pursuit by the underworld demons, his prophetic dream of his own capture, his hiding at his sister's house, and her decision to spend half the time in the underworld in his stead. Both Inanna and Dumuzi's sister Geshtinanna have sympathy and love for him. His "error" in the descent myth is his self-aggrandizement; he does not wear poor clothing and mourn the fallen goddess. It is clearly his overweening arrogance and insensitivity to her trials that cause Inanna unhesitatingly to fix on him the "Eye of Death" that she has won so dearly in the underground.

Some of the derivatives of Dumuzi's name are Damu, Adam, Tammuz, Adonis, Tammerlane, Tam Lin, Tannis, and Thomas. Even this short list, including as it does Sumerian, Babylonian, Scots, Irish, German, Hebrew, Greek, and English heroes, suggests the tremendous dissemination of his story in European folk culture.

As the male god of sacrifice he is in the company of Osiris, Jesus, and others. As the "shepherd king" he is an early version of Paris. In the Sumerian text he has a reed flute; I have substituted a telescope in "The Queen of Swords." On his steppe grows the apple tree of eternal life.

GESHTINANNA: Although at least one source interprets Geshtinanna's volunteering to go down in her brother's stead as the heroic act of a mature woman who has finally learned how to truly and unselfishly love a man, my own experience and study of contemporary therapeutic theory tells me that Geshtinanna is a classic co-alcoholic who cannot let her brother bear his own burdens and the consequences of his actions and attitudes. That she is associated with the fermentation of grain for beer and he is associated with the fermentation of grapes for wine only strengthens my decision to cast her as someone as much in need of Ereshkigal's ministrations as is the arrogant and terrified Dumuzi. Because there is no easy way in our fragmented culture to identify with a brother-sister team, I cast her in "The Queen of Swords" as Thomas's new girlfriend. Nin suggests their original brother-sister relationship in her remark about Hansel and Gretel.

ANNUNAKI and GALLA: The seven judges of Ereshkigal's dominion as well as the seven demons who accompany Inanna to the world above seeking her replacement easily suggested to me the crows that accompany European death-goddesses. That they are also "bar dikes" is simply an addition of modern urban underworld reality and influence. As dissemblers of thought they are a good accompaniment for Ereshkigal's surprisingly sensible approach to teaching Helen/Inanna.

Notes

THE QUEEN OF SWORDS

SCENE ONE

1. Although Inanna's priestesses, notably the great "first poet" Enheduanna and perhaps also the biblical Sarah, were moon-temple officiates, she is so strongly associated with Venus that in later times the goddess of heaven and earth, of life, beauty, and love, came to be called Venus (Roman) and Venus Aphrodite (Roman-Greek). The planet Venus disappears from view for a time as she "descends" to be the morning star or "ascends" to be the evening star again.

GATE ONE

1. The name of Ereshkigal's domain of underworld, or desert, in the Sumerian myth was Ganzir. Here it is represented as a Lesbian bar, the secret meeting place for the underground Gay culture for centuries. The culture owes a great deal to the brave bar owners who provided us with our only means of public expression before the advent of Gay/Lesbian political movements.

2. Ereshkigal's instrument is a "shem drum" in the Sumerian text. I prefer "wind chimes" because of the connection of the wind to the Queen of Swords in the Tarot.

3. Nothing: Neti, the gatekeeper's name in Ereshkigal's domain of Ganzir, translates as "nothing" in Sanskrit.

4. Crows and ravens often accompany the goddess of death in mythology, and represent the world of spirits from the land of the dead. A crow is one of three birds who visited Snow White (a latter-day Inanna) as she lay in her glass casket on the mountain. On the American continent Raven is a trickster figure, especially among Native American tribes of the Northwest.

5. Portrayals of the Queen of Death in later stories associated her with black and red, also the colors of the devouring goddess Kali. Snow White and other derivatives of the Sumerian myth also use the colors red and black. White, of course, is associated with Inanna.

6. Clytemnestra was Helen's sister in the *Iliad*. Clytemnestra murdered her husband on his return from the siege, and was in turn killed by her own son and daughter in a major reversal for the older matriarchal culture; Helen was also killed by the brother and sister, but did not "really" die. Instead she rose into a cloud, her scarf trailing behind her.

7. Priestesses of the temples of Inanna, Ishtar, Astarte, and others had sacred offices whose vestigial characteristics may be found in modern subcultures such as "prostitute" or "dike," "lesbian."

8. "Inner ear" can be translated as "ear wisdom," according to Wolkstein and Kramer in *Inanna, Queen of Heaven and Earth* (see the Additional Readings). Betty De Shong Meador, a Jungian analyst, considers it a reference to intuition or psychic skills: "listen to your inner self."

9. At every gate Inanna starts to question why she is being stripped and is told, "Silence, Inanna. Sacred customs must be obeyed." I suppose this is one reason she does not talk very much in the first half of my play.

10. The wise man Simon Magus and Helen were considered gods and were rivals of Jesus during his lifetime. Peter Fortunato, a poet who played Paris in a staged version of "The Queen of Wands," suggested to me that Simon may have lent his name to Simon Peter. There is a story that Simon Magus attempted to fly in Rome in order to outdo Peter's god.

What I love Simon Magus for is calling Helen she "who stands, has stood, will always stand."

11. The apple of eternal life hung originally on Dumuzi's tree; the goddesses of life and love bestowed it on mortals to guarantee they could safely return to earthly form from the spirit realm. According to Barbara Walker, under Christianity the apple became poisoned, as in the Snow White version of the story, where it is used by the wicked queen to kill Snow White.

GATE TWO

1. "Nature doesn't give a damn" was a fortunate piece of recovery. I had completely forgotten the poem in the tumult of my life. One day while stopping over in Denver I felt compelled to call my friend Francine Kady Butler. We became best friends in 1954 when we were both fourteen, but by 1985 I had been out of touch with her for about ten years. She answered the phone, "Oh, I see you got my ESP." A month before, being unable to find me, she had "put out a message" into the stratosphere, for me to call her. She then sent me a small bundle of my letters and poems from 1960–62, among them "Nature doesn't give a damn." I was in my early twenties then, probably twenty-one when I wrote it.

2. One tradition says that Helen's mother was "Memory"; the other tradition says she was born in the form of an egg from Leda, who had mated

with a swan. A later Greek version said Zeus assumed the form of a swan and raped Leda.

3. In the Sumerian myth "Inanna and the God of Wisdom," Enki is portrayed as an expansive, generous drunk, who confounds himself by giving her all his powers. In still earlier stories Enki "gives birth" and very possibly was a female god at an earlier time.

GATE THREE

Note on the title: *Butch* is a Gay cultural word, stemming from a root word meaning *goat,* and related to sacrificial rites of the great horned god (a version of Dumuzi as the wild bull) of the European Old Religion. Butch and femme are roles in Gay culture that may be played by either gender, with either gender switching at will in all but the most rigid parts of the culture. In ancient ceremonial terms, Butch is the leather-wearing goat-god priest/priestess, either the sacrifice itself or the sacrificer. In some ancient rites the future was read, in a "butcherly" fashion, from the entrails of slain animals sacrificed in the place of the king. Although the sacrifice of a king is considered a male-only office in our historic times, the myth of Inanna's descent makes it clear that the older version of the story began with the idea of female sacrifice—by another female. In more recent times, Joan of Arc has been considered a ceremonial sacrifice, part of an underground pagan culture.

1. *Dike* seemed a more than appropriate title for the Ereshkigal of this story. *Dike* is a Lesbian cultural and lower-class slang word with two distinct roots—one from the lower class and one from the upper. In the former case, *dike* or *dyke* is a shortened version of the name of a queen who fought the Romans, Boudica, whose name was driven underground. Dike as remembered by the literate, upper class was a goddess of Greece. She had both warrior and underworld shamanic qualities. Her name means "natural justice" and her companion was named "Truth." She is portrayed with the wheel of fate, hence the tattoo "Destiny" in the poem. In a latter-day Greek version of the Inanna myth, Dike was softened into Eurydike, or Eurydice, who was held captive against her will in the underworld. Her lover Orpheus (a shepherd-musician like Dumuzi), who went to the underworld to rescue her, looked back at her after having been forbidden to do so, and thus lost her. He then waited for her for seven years on the banks of the Styx before being murdered by maidens.

2. In Gertrude Stein's rendering of the Helen story, "Dr. Faustus Lights the Lights," she characterizes the goddess as "not possibly fooled"—or more exactly, "no one can deceive me."

3. The poem "Descent to the Butch of the Realm" is constructed with three different rhythms. The first I call "Idiomatic Narrative." It consists of

loosely rhythmed and rhymed common American speech pattern lines such as "You won't find me sitting home in front of TV / drinking beer, not me, I'm outdoors. . . ." The second rhythm is a "Tightening Couplet" worked into the fabric of the Idiomatic Narrative. This form is an incomplete sentence, and consists of a couplet in four trochaic or occasionally iambic feet, that rhymes the first two syllables of the first line with the last two syllables of the last line, and contains at least one instance of alliteration, and preferably more. For example: "little yellow egg of being / broken on my greasy griddle." There are nine such tightening couplets in the poem. Their purpose is to pull the looser narrative into a firmer structure so the poem has more tension and "breathes." The third rhythmic form I call "Translation Tablet Chant," based in translations of Sumerian poetry originally written on clay tablets: "Oh descend to me / and my desiring."

GATE FOUR

1. H.D.'s *Helen in Egypt* is based in a variant of the Helen story, according to which only her dream-self, her illusion-shadow, appeared at Troy. Her real self remained in Egypt. (See the Additional Readings.)

SCENE TWO

1. Like *dike, faggot* is a ceremonial Gay word, referring to a history with wands of divination, and then of persecution by burning during the Inquisition. See my book *Another Mother Tongue* (Boston: Beacon Press, 1984) and Arthur Evans, *Witchcraft and the Gay Counterculture* (Boston: Fag Rag Books, 1978).

GATE FIVE

1. Ernest Hemingway, a protégé of Gertrude Stein's for a time, wrote grippingly of bull fighting.
2. The "eye of death" that Ereshkigal fixes on Inanna and that Inanna later fixes on Dumuzi became, in later stories based on it, a mirror of divination, a crystal ball, the surface of a pond—all for the purpose of "seeing with the inner mind," of having psychic or higher-minded knowledge.
3. There is more about warrior queens and Queen Boudica, in particular, in my own book, *Another Mother Tongue*. I based the poem "Queen Boudica" on research I did for that Gay history book.

4. Because of the length and complexity of this poem, for staged production purposes I think it can be heavily trimmed.

5. Crow Dike actresses with physiques different from Ildreth's flaxen North European one may want to substitute for the first stanza one of the following:

All in fur I rode a small horse
deep in the Asian steppe, my hair
so shiny it was black and fine and
down to here.

All in beads I rode, my tall legs
deep in the African grass, my hair
so nappy it was dense and fine and
out to here.

The words *Viking* in the second stanza and *pink* in the third stanza should be changed appropriately.

6. In a staged production the actress may want to substitute her own personal names in the listing of female friends and relatives in order to give the poem a strong subjective dimension.

GATE SIX

1. According to Barbara Walker, the scarecrow is a remnant of rural memory of the Old Religion and the practice of sacrificing the king or substitute king. Perhaps to hang a scarecrow on a peg in the grain fields is to reenact a little bit of the Dumuzi/Inanna myth.

2. This line is a direct quotation from Gertrude Stein.

3. Helen's history in the Greek stories is extremely violent. She was kidnapped by Theseus at the age of nine, and raped. When her twin brothers retrieved her from him, she bore a daughter. This girl, Iphigenia, was given to her older sister Clytemnestra to raise. Later when Helen went to Troy, Clytemnestra's husband Agamemnon could not sail his ships of war out of port because the goddess Artemis had stopped the wind. He sacrificed Iphigenia, who was then about nine herself. In some versions Artemis snatched the girl from death and made her a priestess in her own province.

Helen had a second daughter, Hermione. Inanna appears to have had two sons, each of whom is seized by the Annunaki; Inanna refuses to let them be substituted for herself in the underworld.

4. "Little Snow White," in Grimm's fairy tales, is an incarnation of Helen/Inanna, who swallows a poisoned apple, given to her by an old crone who is actually the "wicked queen," or Ereshkigal. This causes her "death" trance.

5. The House of Horus, the falcon-headed god of Egypt, is also the House of Isis, his mother and a goddess of heaven and earth, similar to Inanna, Ishtar, Astarte, and Demeter. Nephthys, the sister of Isis, ruled the underworld; both goddesses visited the land of the dead in rites for Osiris, the Egyptian god of green plants and sacrifice.

6. The phrase "eating crow" is a euphemism for "eating shit," a reference to the old Native American stories of Raven the Trickster, who keeps people captive by getting them to "eat shit," that is, to endure humiliation and to capitulate to the demands of a more authoritative person. The only escape is to trick Raven into "eating shit" him/herself.

GATE SEVEN

Note on the title: "To reconstitute her, just add water." From *constitute*, to set up, from *status, state*, p.p. of *stare*, to stand. To stand her up again.

This is a very different sense from *resurrection*, from *resurrectus*, from *surge*, to go straight up, to rise, related also to *regere*, to lead straight and *rectus*, right, and *erection*. All of which apply very well to a male god and not, it seems to me, quite so well to a female one.

1. Snow White was put in a glass coffin.

2. The prohibition against eating fruits from the land of the dead, lest one be consigned there forever, is widespread, from the apple of knowledge in Genesis to dozens of folk tales and ballads that warn the hero not to eat what the lady offers.

3. According to Betty Meador, Inanna's colors were carnelian and lapis blue. Gold and white seem always associated with later descriptions, while salmon and blue belong to Mary, who is another version of the queen of heaven and earth.

4. The *me* are powers of godship in ancient Sumer. Inanna acquired them in a mythic text entitled "Inanna and the God of Wisdom" (see Wolkstein and Kramer, *Inanna, Queen of Heaven and Earth*). The word is pronounced *may*, hence the pun "Queen of the May." There were dozens of these powers, from specific priestly rites to such abstractions as "truth," "decision," and "compassion." These qualities stood alongside the power to sack cities, spread discord, use flattering speech, and other characteristics that our culture has separated from the concept of "goodness" and consigned to Ereshkigal rather than to Inanna. Inanna, however, had all of them.

SCENE THREE

1. They *are* Hansel and Gretel. The story of the two children abandoned in the Ganzir of the woods by their evil mother picks up the Sumerian story at the point where Dumuzi and his sister Geshtinanna descend to the domain of death. Ereshkigal, in this medieval folk tale, is represented by both the selfish mother and the boy-eating witch of the woods. Hansel's wits and Gretel's faithful love get them through most of their ordeal, until the moment Gretel kills the witch by tricking her into the oven.

Their names are highly suggestive of the original names, since the suffix *el* is a diminutive meaning "little" or "child." *Gret* retains three out of four letters from *Gesht*inanna, and *Hans* bears auditory resemblance to Thomas, Tam, Tannis, and Tammuz, later versions of Dumuzi's name.

In addition to the most obvious, "Snow White and the Seven Dwarves," other stories from the Grimms' early nineteenth-century collection echo parts of the Inanna/Ereshkigal/Dumuzi saga.

TWO POEMS

DESCENT TO THE ROSES OF THE FAMILY

Nine is the number of transformation, of Uranus the storm god, and of Oya, the warrior goddess of the Macumba religion.

Nine is a major number in "Descent to the Roses of the Family," a poem consisting of nine parts, loosely modeled after the Enneagram, a pattern of nine units that can be read in a linear concentric circle and are also related in a 1-4-2-8-5-7 sequence. So in the poem, sections 5 and 7, for instance, are related by content, since both list characteristics of depression; they are also related by rhythm, both using a form I have named "Translation Tablet Chant."

Additionally the Enneagram structure calls for an internal triad of 3-6-9. So the choral rhythm known as the "Red Rose Chorus" ("nigger is a black core of action / you don't dare take for yourself") occurs in sections 3, 6, and 9, and nowhere else in the poem. Various interpretations of the Enneagram form have been popularized by George Gurdjieff and his followers. Gurdjieff said he had rediscovered the form in a Tibetan monastery.

"Descent to the Roses of the Family" uses five choral styles, or rhythmic/content patterns, in all. For my own purposes I have named them "Idiomatic Narrative," "Tablet Translation Chant," "Red Rose Chorus," "White Rose Chorus," and "Our Father Chant."

The mythic imagery used in "Roses" is from the Inanna descent myth. Snow White and Rose Red are sisters in a European folktale. H.D., in *Helen*

Notes

in Egypt, says that Helen (Inanna) gathered the white rose, and her sister Clytemnestra (Ereshkigal) gathered the red.

The narrator's voice in the poem is a sister addressing her brother on some possible prerequisites for being able to ascend from a family history of being trapped for generations in the underworld of suffering and denial.

TALKERS IN A DREAM DOORWAY

Seven, of course, is the primary number of significance in the Inanna myth, and I would be remiss if I hadn't included a poem based solidly in seven. "Talkers in a Dream Doorway" consists of seven stanzas, of fourteen lines each, divided into thirteen plus one.

Additional Readings

BALLADS AND POETRY

Friedman, Albert B., ed. *The Viking Book of Folk Ballads of the English-Speaking World*. New York: Viking Press, 1956. See especially "Thomas Rymer" and "Tam Lin" (collected by Robert Burns).

H.D. [Hilda Doolittle] *Helen in Egypt*. New York: New Directions, 1961.

Homer. *The Iliad of Homer*. Translated by Richmond Lattimore. Chicago: University of Chicago Press, 1977. The saga of Paris and Helen.

Kinsley, James, ed. *The Oxford Book of Ballads*. Oxford: Clarendon Press, 1982. Versions of "Thomas the Rhymer," "Tam Lin," "Hind Etin," and also "King Orfeo."

Leach, MacEdward, ed. *The Ballad Book*. New York: Harper and Brothers, 1955. Versions of "Thomas Rymer," "Tam Lin," and "Hind Etin."

Spiers, John. *Medieval English Poetry: The Non-Chaucerian Tradition*. London: Faber and Faber, 1975. See especially "Thomas of Ercildoune and the Quene of Elfland."

Stein, Gertrude. "Dr. Faustus Lights the Lights." In *Last Operas and Plays*. New York: Vintage Books, 1975.

STORIES

Grimm, Jacob, and Wilhelm K. Grimm. *The Complete Fairy Tales of the Brothers Grimm*. Translated by Jack Zipes. New York: Bantam Books, 1987.

————. *The Juniper Tree and Other Tales from Grimm*. Translated by Lore Segal and Randall Jarrell. New York: Farrar, Straus, and Giroux, 1973. See especially "Snow White and the Seven Dwarves," "Hansel and Gretel," "The Juniper Tree," "The Poor Miller's Boy and the Little Cat," "The Two Journeymen," and "Bearskin."

SUMERIAN INANNA TEXTS AND INTERPRETATIONS

Meador, Betty De Shong. "Descent of the Goddess Inanna to the Underworld." Oakland, Calif.: Inanna Institute, Box 11164, Oakland, Calif.,
94611. 1987. Poetry based on the Sumerian cuneiform text.

———. "Poems of Enheduanna, High Priestess, Poet and Prophet of the
Moon Temple of Sumer." Unpublished manuscript.

Perera, Sylvia Brinton. *Descent to the Goddess: A Way of Initiation for Women.*
Toronto: Inner City Books, 1981.

Wolkstein, Diane, and Samuel Noah Kramer. *Inanna, Queen of Heaven and
Earth: Her Stories and Hymns from Sumer.* New York: Harper and Row,
1983.

GENERAL SOURCES

Teubal, Savina J. *Sarah the Priestess: The First Matriarch of Genesis.* Athens,
Ohio: Swallow Press, 1984.

Walker, Barbara G. *The Women's Encyclopedia of Myths and Secrets.* San
Francisco: Harper and Row, 1983.